THE HOLIDAY CAMPERS

The Holiday Campers

Petra Christian

NEW ENGLISH LIBRARY
TIMES MIRROR

To My Father
I thought he was an uncle

PROLOGUE

I WAS 21. In Paris I nearly got sold as a white slave. In Nice I became a whore. In Greece I smuggled drugs. In Sweden I made blue films. In Morocco I became a *kif*-head until the police broke it up.*

And I thought travel broadened the mind. . . .

When I landed at London Airport on my way back from Morocco, I knew one thing with a stunning certitude: I wanted no more of it. In just 18 months of my life I had crammed in enough adventures to last anyone a lifetime. But they were not pleasant memories. Somehow, although I had felt I was enjoying myself at the time, I felt sickened to the core. I had been halfway round Europe, and the strongest memory I had was a recurring image of bedroom ceilings, viewed from below.

And so. . . . Dear old London – smelly, dirty, *normal* – welcomed me back to its embrace. I moved into a bedsitter, got myself a job, and tried to forget the past.

The trouble was, it wouldn't forget me. I didn't realise it at the time, because I couldn't recognise it, but my exotic experiences were still lurking in my subconscious.

The first clue I had I mistook for something else entirely. I woke up one morning feeling as sick as a pig. I made it to the loo with a few seconds to spare, and *was* as sick as a pig. Afterwards, feeling drained and washed out, the only cause I could attribute to it was that I must be pregnant. That didn't make sense, because I'd been on the pill since the 5th Form. Unless some fun-loving prankster had done a quiet swap. . . . I checked my supply, but it didn't seem possible. You're always hearing about people swapping birth-pills for aspirin, but it's almost impossible to do. Each pill is sealed in a special compartment, and if anyone had tampered with them you'd *know*.

So . . . I attributed the sickness to something I must have eaten the night before, and that was that.

Lunchtime of that day, though, I got the most violent headache of my life. The boss sent me home, and I spent the rest of the day in bed.

* See *Hitch-Hiker* (1971) and *The New Drifters* (1972) by Petra Christian, New English Library.

The next morning I was sick again, and went to the doctor. 'You're just run down, Miss Deenes,' said my friendly neighbourhood GP, scribbling on his pad. 'Take these three times a day, next please. . . . '

The pills didn't help. I found I could not sleep, and the headaches continued. Everything I ate was thrown up. I began to get aches and pains in my back, and I lost weight. Now getting really scared, I went to another doctor. More run-down-in-need-of-a-tonic pills, and the headaches, nausea, insomnia went on as before.

I grew very nervous, and jumped at the slightest surprise. I was irritable, and snapped at everybody.

Then one night, I lay in my bed, trying to sleep, and an immense fear grew in me. It was the more frightening for being undefined. I tried to control it: switched on the light, tried to read. But it was still there. I looked round at the walls, at the ceiling. They seemed closer, the room was hot, the bed was moist and swallowing me, there was a dark shadow by the cupboard, a noise in the corridor outside. A car went by in the street below, and the noise sounded like a clap of thunder. I ran to the window, snatched back the curtains. There were two men in the street, walking quickly away. They had been there just now. . . . I turned back to the room, which was smaller and hotter than before. I turned on all the lights, but the darkness remained. I drank a glass of water, but it tasted foul and dirty. I stumbled over a chair, fell to the floor, feeling the tufty texture of the carpet as if it were a million tiny needles. With shaking hands, I put on a record, turned the volume to its loudest.

And then I started to scream. . . .

And scream, and scream. . . .

After a few moments the door was knocked down from outside, and two men burst in. They were wearing pyjamas, and my terror redoubled. I screamed and screamed, fighting desperately with them as they tried to pull me to my feet. I snatched at one man's hair, clawed at the other man's eyes. I was naked, and I felt their hands on my body. Nausea welled in me, and my screams were stayed while I vomited. Then I started again, uncaring that the sick was all over my body. The men tried again, lifting me, pulling me, touching me. . . . I swung at them, trying to fight them off, trying to kill them. Then a woman appeared, and I appealed to her to help . . . but she came to the men and then her hands were on me.

I was on my feet now, pressed against a wall. I kicked, spat, fought. I caught one of the men on the ear, tearing his flesh. He ducked away, holding the side of his head. Then he came back and raised his hand. His fingers were bunched into a fist. . . .

I lay in the bed, and saw that my name was Deenes, Sally (Miss). There was a curtain round the bed, and beside me there was a low table which held a couple of paperbacks, a bowl of fruit, a bottle of Lucozade, some Kleenex, a radio and a tumbler. Every hour or so a nurse would pop in to see me, fluff up my pillows and ask me if I needed anything. I never did.

Then there were the doctors. There were two. One was young, and rather abrupt with me. He only came once or twice. Then there was the other one: middle-aged and Indian, he was kindness itself to me. But the odd thing was, he never seemed to ask me about my health. All he did was talk to me.

I had visitors. Several friends came, and Mum and Dad. All wanted to know what had happened . . . and I couldn't tell them. I hadn't the faintest idea. I remembered freaking out in the bedsitter, sure enough, but why, I had no idea.

The only words I knew were two that I would never have thought would apply to me: nervous breakdown.

I also had a condition known in the trade as amnesia . . . loss of memory. I don't recommend it. It's like standing in front of a big white sheet, behind which could be anything on Earth.

But this was a long and depressing episode; I don't want to dwell on it. The recollection is a painful one, and is no pleasure to recount.

Suffice it to say, then, that I was in hospital for a month. During that time I was under sedation for at least two weeks. Then, I had remedial therapy, which was supposed to help me come to grips with the world.

By the time I left hospital, a large part of my memory had returned. I remembered my childhood, and my schooldays. I remembered my first few jobs, and I recognised my friends. But the part of my life which began when I upped and went was a blank to me. I was still well and truly in the grips of the trauma.

Even so, I was able to live a relatively normal life. I left my bedsitter, of course, and went back home to live with my parents. I had to take pills to keep me from getting excited, I was not allowed to work and I was told very gently that boyfriends were to be discouraged.

Gradually, I got used to the idea of having lost 18 months of my life. It wasn't exactly fun, but you can live with anything in time.

7

Mum did everything in her power to help me remember, but it was no good.

'See this card, Sal,' she'd say, thrusting a bit of highly-coloured postcard into my hands. 'You sent me that from Nice.'

I'd look at it. A strange town, a long way away. On the back, my scribbly handwriting, talking about a job I was hoping to get. It meant nothing to me.

'So you say I went abroad?' I kept asking.

'That's what you told us. "I'm off for a short holiday," you said, and that was the last we saw of you.'

I would stare at those postcards for hours, hoping they'd trigger off some deeply-buried memory. But there was nothing there. Whatever had happened must have run deep and strong inside me.

I was not yet completely released from medical supervision. After all, a girl with amnesia is technically very ill, even if she is in otherwise roaring good health. I had to call in once a week to my GP, and get him to OK me that I was still physically fit, and not likely to relapse into nervous collapse.

And once a week I was sent for mental therapy to a psychiatrist.

When I was first told, I was frightened, then amused and then bored. I was frightened because I'd never been to a head-shrinker in my life, and didn't know what it would involve. I was amused, because I had a sudden mental image of a tall German with lorgnettes and a gold watch-chain, hypnotising me and smudging ink on bits of paper. And then I was bored, because I couldn't think of anything I'd like to do less than lie on some couch and talk about myself.

So I turned up for my first appointment with a distinct mixture of feelings.

Dad dropped me off at the corner of Harley Street, and I walked along slowly until I came to the house. I was clutching my letter the hospital had written for me. Without that, I'd never get in, because if it weren't for the Good-Old-National-Health I'd never have been able to afford it.

I rang the bell. After a moment, a woman answered it.

'Yes?'

'Is the doctor in?'

'Is he expecting you?'

'Yes.' The woman glared at me. 'It's Miss Deenes.'

'Oh yes. You'd better come in.'

I was conducted inside, and my coat was hung on a stand. She led me to a flight of stairs, and we began to walk up. The woman moved with slow, precise steps, taking only one stair at a time even though the gradient was very shallow. If I'd been on my own, the tomboy in me would have sent me hurtling up three at a time.

On the first landing we passed an open door. I glanced through it. Inside the room was a desk, and a couch. My stomach lurched. There was something so cold and clinical about it. I was about to be turned inside out.

We carried on to the next floor, and here I was taken into a large, and brightly-lit room. At first I thought it must be the doctor's living quarters, for the furnishings were so informal, but there was none of the kind of impedimenta you see around a house. It was all too carefully arranged.

In one corner was a large, leather-topped desk. I had time only to see a framed photograph of a young, attractive woman and two happy children, when the nurse said: 'The doctor will see you in a moment.'

She went out of the door, closing it behind her. An instant later, another door opened, and the doctor came in.

I looked at him incuriously. He was no longer young, not yet middle-aged. Thirty-two I guessed, though this estimate was largely an involuntary act on my behalf. I was not assessing him. His hair was short, and well-groomed. He wore a pale-brown suit, a flower in a button-hole and a tie of exquisite good taste and a perfect match to his shirt and suit.

He nodded to me, sat at the other side of the desk and the treatment began.

That first session was rather disappointing. All he did was to ask me many questions about myself ... some formal ones, others rather more intimate. To each of my answers he nodded gravely, and wrote at length on to a large pad of paper in front of him.

At the end of the questions he stood up, and extended his hand.

'Thank you, Miss Deenes.' I shook his hand, and retrieved my letter of introduction.

'Is that all, doctor?'

'For this week, yes. Fix an appointment with the nurse on your way out. This time next week, I think?'

I nodded. I had nothing else to do.

As I closed the door, my last sight of him was sitting at his desk, the photograph of the woman and children (his wife? his kids?) at his side. He was writing diligently on to his pad.

The second session was more obviously concerned with my

amnesia. He asked me many questions about my childhood, and tried to trap me into talking about my lost 18 months. But it was no good. I genuinely had no recollection of them at all.

At the end of that session, he said: 'Well, Miss Deenes. I now have a clear idea of what you were like before your period of amnesia began. By looking at you, and talking to you, I have a good idea of what you are like now. The problem remains to fill in the gap. That's what we shall start next week.'

So it was with a sure knowledge that my mind was about to be invaded that I turned up the following week.

This time, I was led through his office, and into an inner room. One I had not seen before.

'This is my consulting-room,' he said.

I stared at it in fascination.

It was nothing like I would have imagined. It was more like a study or library in an old country house, than a psychiatric consulting-room. Two of the four walls were lined with books. A colour television-set was in one corner, and beside it a well-stocked cocktail bar. There was a stack of records on a table, and beside it an expensive hi-fi kit. The floor was lushly carpeted.

'Please make yourself comfortable, Miss Deenes. Let me take your coat.'

He nodded towards a bright-blue couch, and after I had given him my coat I went and sat down. Almost immediately, I jumped up again!

It had felt as if I was sinking in water.

'Is there something wrong?'

'Your couch . . . it feels funny.'

The doctor laughed. 'Don't worry. It's perfectly safe. It's a water-bed. I bought it last year when I was in America. Lie down on it, make yourself comfortable. I promise you that you will have never felt anything like it before in your life.'

He couldn't have been more right. I lay back on the blue cover, half expecting a deluge of water to rise up from between my legs . . . but no, I just sank back and back and back. . . .

It felt as if I were floating. The illusion was so good that I could hardly feel where my body touched against the cover.

'You like it?'

'Yes.'

'So do most of my patients.'

'But I thought I saw your consulting-room downstairs.'

'You did. That's the one I use for the – shall we say – more conservative of my patients?'

'I vote Labour,' I said.

'Good.' The doctor pulled up a stool from the cocktail bar, and sat on it slightly behind me. He pulled forward a clipboard and took a ballpoint pen from his pocket.

'Are you comfortable?'

'Put it this way,' I said. 'If you don't start asking me questions, I'll be asleep.'

'Good. It's essential that you relax.'

'I'm relaxing,' I said, closing my eyes and imagining I was lying on a cloud, approximately one thousand feet above a South Pacific Island.

'I'm afraid I must ask you more questions about your past. Answer them impulsively. Don't leave anything out, however irrelevant it may seem to you. If you don't know the answer, say so.'

'OK.'

And so the questions began. I found there were a lot of don't-knows. In fact, it soon became pretty clear that the 18-month blank was as solid as ever. That session achieved nothing, and neither did any of the next three that followed.

The impression I was getting reminded me of something I *could* remember from my past. When I was a child, I'd done some painting using a candle. The idea was that you 'wrote' on paper by rubbing the end of a candle across it, then painted away like mad with water paints. When you had finished, you had a mass of colour with a lot of white squiggles where the candle has been.

I was beginning to see my amnesia like that. The more questions I could answer for the doctor, the clearer my past before the amnesia became. The more I got around, the clearer my present became. And consequently, the white spot where the candle of my amnesia was, stood out in clearer relief.

I began to think I would never be able to paint in the details.

Then, on the fifth consultation where I lay on that dreamily-soft water-bed, something happened to trigger a memory.

By this time, the doctor and I were on first-name terms. This doesn't mean we were becoming closer friends, but that Trevor had said that a form of intimacy between us would make it easier for me to talk about myself. It seemed true enough.

The breakthrough came like this. I was nearing the end of the fifth session. As usual, I lay on the water-bed, while Trevor sat behind me on his stool. I was telling him about life at school. Then he said:

'Did you experience any traumae at school?'

'Traumae?'

'Very strong emotional experiences. Something that might have shocked you, or frightened you, or affected your relationships with people.'

'Could you give me an example?'

'Well . . . suppose you were pregnant, for example. You may choose to have an abortion, if you were unmarried. For some women, having an abortion can be a deeply disturbing experience.'

'I see,' I said, but all of a sudden my mind was drifting away. It was that word 'abortion'. The trigger had been touched. It summoned an image in my mind, but at first I couldn't locate or identify it.

I must have closed my eyes, or slumped back, for Trevor noticed the change.

'I've said something which has keyed you,' he said. 'Don't try to fight it. Drift with it.'

I was hardly listening to him. I was thinking about an abortion . . . one which I had had.

And yet . . . I said nothing. The memory was a dreamlike one, in the way that a nightmare will return to you in your waking hours, still chilling you even though you know it was never real.

There was a blankness in my memory, and now here was a key to that memory. I had been pregnant, and I had an abortion. But that had never happened to me! Was it a real memory, or was it a fantasy? It seemed real, and yet not true. A fact, but a created fact.

'I think . . .'

'You have something?' Trevor said quickly.

'I'm not sure.'

'Let it take you over. However unreal it might seem to you, it will help us retrieve your memory. Formalise it in your mind, then tell me what it is.'

'I'm trying, I'm trying . . .'

I had my eyes tightly closed, thinking about the agony of the abortion, the shame. I saw my mother's face for an instant, scolding me; but it was not Mum, not the Mum I knew. It seemed to be another woman, yet someone who was still 'Mother' to me. And the sensation I had was of myself, yet not of myself. It was very confusing.

I was constructing an identity in my mind . . . and a sequence of events. They were real – oh my God! how real they seemed! – and yet I knew too with an overwhelming compulsion that they were untrue. They had happened, and they had happened to me, but were they the memories I had lost?

'An abortion . . . ' I said slowly. 'I have had an abortion.'

'Tell me about it.'

'No . . . I can't see it . . .'

I was aware that Trevor had moved away from me. A few seconds later he was back. I opened my eyes. He was holding a glass of water and two little yellow pills.

'Take these,' he said. 'They will help your mind formalise. They are completely harmless.'

Obediently, I took the pills and swallowed them.

Trevor was looking at his watch.

'Now listen, Sally. Your consultation is nearly over. But this is very interesting. I feel as if we are on the brink of a breakthrough.'

'Do I have to go?'

'Not if you don't want to. I have one more patient to see, and she is probably waiting for me now. Can you stay here for a little while longer?'

I nodded.

'Good.' He glanced at his watch again. 'I'll telephone your mother, and tell her you'll be a little later than usual. Then I'll get rid of the other patient, and you can tell me what's in your memory.'

He stood up, and hurried from the consulting room.

I lay back on the water-bed, staring into space. It was making more sense now. Perhaps it was the pills, perhaps it was the memory returning. False or otherwise, it was all I had. I clung to it desperately. Images came swimming up in my mind.

. . . a row of tiny wooden buildings. . . .

. . . a bright-blue pool, full of laughing people. . . .

. . . a band, playing 'Smoke Gets In Your Eyes'. . . .

. . . a motorbike. . . .

. . . two middle-aged men, wheezing with laughter. . . .

They were making sense. They were not memories that were mine, but they were real, so real. I wanted them, demanded them.

And slowly, they began to slot into order.

Formalise them, Trevor had said. *However unreal, they will help. . . .*

Half-formed, they hung in my memory. It was a pleasant experience. If you don't think so, you probably haven't had amnesia. Memory is something most people take for granted. This was a memory, it was mine, and I was going to have it.

Trevor came back in. He closed the door, and sat down again on his stool.

'OK, Sally. You've got all the time in the world. Why not tell me about your abortion?'

I shook my head.

'No abortion. It happened . . . but it is not important. I remember now. It was what the abortion made me do . . . a new life. That's what happened.'

And then the memories slotted into a logical order. I settled down on the water-bed, closed my eyes and let the newly-discovered cinema in my mind show me pictures. I looked at them . . . and described them to Trevor.

Slowly, the memory became a story, and then it became a part of my life.

Not mine. . . .

But *real*. . . .

CHAPTER 1

THE train rolled westwards. It was raining, and droplets skidded across the outside of the glass at an almost horizontal angle, but I could see ahead, when the train went into a bend, that the sky was clearer. It was one hell of a time to be going to the seaside, and if I hadn't had the letter and the cheque a couple of days before I don't think I would have got as far as the station.

Anyway, the brightening sky seemed to be a good omen, though North Devon in April can be as cold as Trondheim in a gale. Why Porter's Sunnynook? I kept asking myself. With a name like that, it didn't deserve to make it into the holiday-guides even. Nevertheless, it existed and it was real. Actually, I did know the reason why it was Sunnynook instead of any one of a hundred others: many years ago, when I was a small child, I had been there for a week with my parents.

My memory of that week was one of unbroken sunshine, a fabulous paddling-pool and endless sandcastles on the private beach.

Things had changed of course. That faint stiffness in my back, for instance. Now the only reminder I had of the tiny life I had carried in me for a few weeks. And of course, a reminder of Paul and his so-desirable personality.

I had been so *naive*! I had fallen for him like a ton of bricks, been taken in by him . . . and almost destroyed by him. Looking back, I had to gulp at his breathtaking arrogance, and sheer panache. The things he got me to swallow! I believed him, for instance, when he told me he was taking a male Pill, so sex would be 'all right'. I believed him when I missed a period and he said it was the high-pressure zone over London at that time. I believed him the following month when I finally twigged that I had one on the way, and he told me that he must have 'forgotten' to take his mythical Pill once or twice. And worst of all, I believed him when he said he'd marry me.

I suppose the ring helped me along with that belief, but even that didn't satisfy me – at long bloody last – of his bona fides the night I called round on him unexpectedly, and found him romping round his flat in the nude. With Brenda. My best friend.

To cut a long and not very pleasant story short, I blued my savings (yes, I'd fallen for the saving-up-to-get-married thing too) and bought myself a National Health abortion, threw his ring into the deepest river I could find, and looked round for something else to do.

If that sounds flip, it isn't. I was beginning to feel like a girl in one of those kitchen-sink sagas that were so popular a few years ago. You know, boring background, lousy boyfriend, abortion, etc., etc. It was all too real and tragic for my liking. I was 19, and all I wanted was a good healthy dose of escapist fantasy.

It was with this realisation that the idea about Porters Sunnynook came to light.

There is something about a holiday-camp that appeals to the escapist in us all. A little world, cut off from everywhere else. Self-sufficient. A different set of rules apply. No one has to be themselves. The problems outside can be ignored for a couple of weeks.

All the appeal of a foreign country, but the natives speak English.

So why not get a job in one?

Once the idea had taken root, I couldn't be turned back from it. The job I was in was diabolical, and the people I worked with knew a lot about what had happened between Paul and me. For that reason alone, I wanted a change.

Porter's Sunnynook became the obvious choice. I knew it from old, and I didn't want somewhere too big. Sunnynook was a small, family camp, built on a wooded hill overlooking the sea.

I rooted through an old trunk, and after about an hour's search managed to find the old brochure we had had when we went so many years before.

I found the phone-number, rang them up and – yes – they were hiring staff at that time for the summer season. I sent them a photograph of myself, and a couple of days later received a letter saying I had been hired and would I turn up for duty the the following Monday.

So here I was, sitting on British Rail Inter-City, looking for ward to a few months of sheer escapism.

I changed trains in Exeter, and about an hour later the little local train pulled into the station. I dragged my portable home – two suitcases – from the rack, and walked through the barrier into the station yard. Two taxis stood there waiting, and I walked to the first one.

'Porter's Sunnynook, please,' I said.

The taxi-driver stared at me blankly.

'Where, miss?'

'Sunnynook. The holiday camp.'

'There's nowhere here of that name.'

I looked at him in mild alarm.

'But . . . surely. They must be here. I wrote to them, spoke to them on the phone.'

'A holiday camp, you say? There's only one here. . . .' The man frowned. 'Wait a minute, you said Sunnynook?'

I nodded eagerly.

'That rings a bell. Ah yes, of course. I'm afraid you're living in the past a bit. They changed hands years ago. Not called that any more. A big American company bought it from old Porter, and they've modernised it a lot. It's called Priest's Cave Holiday Centre now.'

'Priest's Cave?'

'Yeah. They bought some extra land to build on, and they found a series of caves in the cliff. Apparently, they were where the priests used to hide during the persecution, before being shipped over to Ireland.'

'But it's the same place?'

'Yes.' He looked at me quizzically. 'A bit early, aren't you? There won't be much going on there for a week or two. The season's not really started.'

'Oh, I'm not going on holiday,' I said. 'I'm working there.'

The driver's expression changed. He winked at me.

'I see. Sorry, I didn't think you looked the type.'

I looked at him questioningly, but he picked up my cases and stowed them in the boot. I climbed into the cab, and waited while he started the engine and drove out of the yard and along the road into town.

I sat in silence as we cruised along the sea-front, and then up a winding road leading towards a hill. The camp appeared to be a long way from the centre of town, further in fact than I remembered.

After about five minutes we arrived at the camp . . . and what a difference!

As I remembered it, there were about fifty rustic wooden chalets, dotted discreetly among the trees, with one central block containing the restaurant, etc. But now it was like a small town in its own right. Most of the trees had been felled, and the chalets were painted in bright, gaudy colours. The central building was still there, but now it was adorned with banners, flags and coloured lights. In the drab light of that April afternoon the whole place looked like a shanty town which had fallen on hard times, and had then been repainted.

Over the main door was a painted sign: *Welcome to Priest's Cave Holiday Centre.*

This, undoubtedly, was it.

The cab-driver stopped the taxi outside the reception office, opened the door for me and carried my bags up the steps. I fished in my purse.

'How much do I owe you?'

He grinned.

'Forget it . . . for now, anyway. We'll be seeing each other. This is a small town, and like I said this is the only holiday camp. Not too many taxi drivers around, either. So as I say, we'll be seeing each other. Soon as things get going, and you've learned the score, we'll be able to help each other out quite a bit. The name's Dave, by the way.'

I was more than a little mystified. Still, who was I to argue? I thanked him, picked up my cases and humped them in to the reception.

'I'd like to see the personnel-manager,' I said to a bored-looking girl behind the desk.

She worked her piece of chewing-gum into a corner of her mouth, and pointed down a corridor.

'Over there,' she said. 'Third door from the end.'

I walked along until I reached the indicated door. A plate on the door said: *Alan Spiers, Personnel Admin.* I knocked.

'Come in!'

I opened the door, and went inside.

'I'm Sally Deenes,' I said. 'I'm due to report for work today.'

Alan Spiers was much younger than I had expected him to be. He was in his late 20s, and looked more like a civilised hippy than an office type. He rummaged in a drawer of his desk and pulled out a sheaf of correspondence.

'Deenes . . . Sally Deenes,' he muttered, flipping through the forms. 'Oh yes, here we are.'

He read through my letter again quickly, looking up from time to time to glance at me. He had the same puzzled look in his face as the taxi-driver's.

'Ever done this sort of work before?'

'No,' I said.

'Ah . . . then that would explain it. You don't look like one of the old timers.'

Nothing like a compliment to a 19-year old.

'Right then,' he said, putting aside my letter. 'First things first. My name is Alan Spiers, and my job is to look after the staff and keep things under control. If you have any problems, you come to me first. I think that's it . . . you'll pick up the routine from the other girls. Would you like to see your living quarters?'

I nodded, marvelling to myself at the comprehensiveness of the interview. Everything you need to know about work in a holiday camp in under ten seconds.

We left the central building and walked slowly up the hill. Alan Spiers carried one of my bags, and for that I was grateful. We passed an amusement arcade, and a games-room, then up past a boarded-up shop and into the chalets. These had been built in straight lines, stretching away from one side to the other, almost as far as the eye could see. I began to think that the chalets went on for ever up the hill, but in the end we were through them and were walking across a relatively flat patch of ground that was marked out as a football field. Beyond this, we walked down a winding path.

'A long way from the centre of things, isn't it?' I said.

'You'll soon get used to it. It only seems a long way at first.'

We rounded a bend in the path, and suddenly I saw the 'living quarters' that he had mentioned. When I had my first impression of the whole camp it was of a shanty-town . . . but I was wrong. *This* was the shanty-town. There was a sprawling collection of drab-grey prefabricated huts which looked as if they had been custom-built for war-refugees.

Alan Spiers led the way to a long low hut.

'You sleep dormitory-style,' he explained, climbing up the steps. 'These are the female quarters, and the male quarters are on the other side.'

We went inside the hut. The interior was a shambles, with about two dozen beds lined up against one wall and a random collection of cupboards and storage lockers against the other.

There were four girls in the hut; three sitting together at the far end, talking and laughing, and the other lying by herself on one of the beds, reading a magazine. Alan led me to the bed next to hers.

'Here . . . this will do you,' he said. 'Help yourself to locker-space where you can find it. You'll have to haggle with the other girls for blankets and sheets and things. We bring the whole lot in every Monday morning and you'll have to work out your own schedules for cleaning the hut and things like that.'

He turned to the girl lying on the bed.

'Doreen . . . this is Sally Deenes. She's new. Fill her in on all the relevant details, will you? I've got to get back to reception.'

She sat up, apparently unconcerned that her dressing-gown was undone down the front and most of one breast peeked through.

'Hi, Sally.'

'Hello.'

'Good . . . so you're old friends now. Doreen will give you all the dope, Sally. I'll come to some decision about shifts later. See you.'

He walked out of the hut, smiling in a way that I felt was not a friendly gesture but a way of providing himself with an exit-line.

Doreen looked at me, and smiled in a not unfriendly way.

'Is this your first time in a camp?'

'Yes, it is.'

'Well, don't worry. It's not as bad as you think. You'll soon be one of us. I'm a veteran.'

Don't worry? Not as bad? A veteran? She was making it sound like two years hard labour.

She offered me a cigarette, which I accepted gratefully.

'What are you doing?'

'The letter I got said general duties.'

Doreen nodded.

'Yes. You're the same as me then, love. And most of the others. That means you'll be doing anything from serving in the restau-

19

rant, doing night patrol work, looking after the children's day nursery or judging the knobbly-knees competition.'

'They have those here?'

'Dead right they do. And that's not the worst. You should see the pot-belly contest on the last night.'

'I think I'll skip that.'

'That's what I thought,' said Doreen. 'But last year I had to actually measure them one week.'

'Ugh!' I drew on my cigarette, welcoming the feeling of normality it gave me. 'Between all this work, do we get any time off?'

Doreen laughed.

'Don't worry. You'll get plenty of time to do the important things.'

'I'm sorry,' I said. 'But I don't quite follow you.'

Doreen stared at me incredulously.

'My God, Sally,' she said. 'You really are new to this job, aren't you?'

I must have looked pretty blank.

'Listen, love,' said Doreen in a confidential voice. 'How much are you getting paid for this job?'

'Eight pounds clear,' I said. 'But we get free food, drinks and accommodation.'

'That's enough for you?'

'Well, there isn't much to spend money on here.'

'Would you believe me if I told you that by the end of the season you'll probably have saved up at least £600?'

'Not really. It isn't possible. Not out of £8 a week.'

'I just don't believe it,' said Doreen in astonishment. 'Are you really so innocent, or are you putting me on?'

'Honestly,' I said. 'I don't know what you mean.'

'I think,' said Doreen, looking round the almost deserted hut, 'that it is time someone put you straight about the facts of life in this place. And that someone might as well be me.'

CHAPTER 2

DOREEN looked at me pragmatically.

'For a start-off,' she said, 'why do you think people come to this camp?'

It was too easy. 'For a holiday?'

It was too easy. Doreen smiled indulgently.

'From the washed-out look of some of them leaving this place at the end of their fortnight you'd think a holiday was the last thing they'd been having. Some blokes come here for two weeks, and spend the next month at a health-farm trying to get their strength back.'

'It's not . . .?' My voice tailed off. 'It's not . . . one of those camps where everything's very regimentated, is it?'

'You could put it that way.'

'Then why do they come?'

'To enjoy themselves. For Mum, Dad and Gran, that means watching the camp-concerts, lazing around the swimming-pool and old-time dancing at night. But the young blokes who come here have their eyes set on a very different sort of entertainment.'

I felt a sort of nudging in my mind.

'Not. . . .?'

Doreen grinned broadly. 'That's right. Us.'

'We . . . supply the entertainment.'

'That's right. I knew you'd catch on. Of course, you don't have to take part, but you'll find that eight quid a week doesn't go very far, even when your keep is being paid.'

'But, I . . . I've never. . . .'

'Don't worry. You don't have to work at it. You'll get plenty of offers, and Alan Spiers will sometimes pass on a few useful contacts once he gets to trust you.'

'So our personnel manager does double duty as a pimp?' The flat, matter-of-fact tone of Doreen's voice was having quite the opposite effect on me: I couldn't take her seriously. My answer was intended to be sarcastic, but it floated right over the top of her head.

'Well, he's not really a pimp,' she said quite seriously. 'I mean, he doesn't expect a cut or anything. He gets his bunce from the customers. A sort of direct selling fee.'

'And where do these nefarious activities take place?'

'Usually in the customer's chalet. It's best there. Technically, a girl can get the sack for bringing a mark here, but in practice the management will turn a blind eye. No, the real reason is that it's just not private enough. Anyway, the security-patrols like to know where the action is at any given moment.'

'The security-staff are in on it too?' The whole business was beginning to take on the proportions of a gigantic international vice racket.

'Oh yes. We couldn't really do it without their help. Mind you – you'll have to slip them something from time to time. We usually give the bloke on duty a fiver a night. We have a whip-round for it as we come off restaurant-duty in the evenings.'

I did a quick mental calculation. I imagined that being a security-officer was one of the better-paid jobs on the camp. Say they got £20 a week, then they'd add another £30 or £35 from this source. Nice line to be in.

'Pretty good money for doing nothing,' I said.

Doreen shook her head.

'Oh no, the security boys really do earn their money. Most of them get beaten up at least once in a season . . . and anyway, they do us a service by putting off the enthusiastic amateurs.'

'Amateurs?'

'Single girls come here too. They're out for a good time, and you wouldn't believe the tricks these birds will get up to once they're away from Mum, Dad and the boyfriend. Disgraceful, I call it. No morals at all. Well, the security-patrols are supposed to prevent that. They've got pass-keys to all the chalets, you see.'

I stared at Doreen, and then burst out laughing. I couldn't help it. There she was expounding the ins and outs of prostitution, and being seriously shocked by ordinary girls looking out for a bit of fun. It was, as I was to discover, typical of the double set of values which applied in the closeted world of the camp.

I think Doreen was about to instruct me in the usual rates of payment and fees for specialist services, so I thought it was time to cut out of the conversation.

'Look, Doreen,' I said gently. 'I really do appreciate your trying to help me, but I don't think I want to be involved, thanks all the same. Believe it or not, I came to work here purely as a way of getting away from home for a few months. Eight quid a week will suit me fine.'

Doreen looked baffled.

'Please yourself,' she said. 'I think you're bloody mad, but that's your funeral.'

'Maybe I am,' I said. 'But that's the way I want it to be.'

Doreen looked at me thoughtfully.

'Here,' she said. 'You won't rock the boat for the rest of us, will you?'

'No . . . I'm not like that. I don't exactly approve, but if you and the rest want to do it, it's up to you.'

Doreen grinned. At first, I thought it was a grin of relief, but then I thought I detected an element of real good humour.

Impulsively, she reached out and squeezed my hand. It was the first sign I had seen that she was warm . . . not just the hardened, holiday-camp whore she made herself out to be. I found myself wondering just how much of a front it was. Perhaps it was her way of telling me that life at Priest's Cave was not going to be the idyll I had thought.

Even so, the camp was going to serve its purpose, however bad or hard the life might turn out to be. It was that tiny world I sought, an artificial abstraction removed from the various unpleasantnesses of real life.

During the next week I gradually slipped in to the tempo of camp life.

We had to start early: being awakened at six. The first thing we had to do was tidy up the dormitory (a task which was generally neglected) and report for duty to the staff supervision office at seven. There was a complicated shift scheme for breakfast, which coincided with several chores around the camp. At eight, the campers' breakfasts began and although there were no guests there that week we were shown the drill. Some helped in the kitchens, others filled in in the restaurant. After breakfast we were each given an hour off, in which we could do as we liked. This again was organised on a shift-system. Work was to continue like this throughout the day. Of course, in that first week everything was a dummy-run, and it was more to familiarise ourselves with the lay-out of the camp, meet the various supervisors, learn the drill for such emergencies as accidents in the swimming-pool, fires and so on.

Once or twice we were given short lectures by Alan Spiers, who drummed it into our heads that the guests were here on holiday, and that we had to do anything and everything to make sure they enjoyed themselves. Though Doreen nudged me meaningfully when he said this, there was no hint or implication from him to confirm what she had told me that first day. Everything seemed to be entirely above board.

Possibly the only thing which lent a semblance of truth to her words was the uniform we were issued with. This was very attractive, and I was pleased with it. It consisted of a white mini-skirt and pale-blue blouse, made of semi-transparent material. If the weather grew colder, we were allowed to wear a dark-blue blazer over the blouse.

We tried on the uniforms in the hut, and Doreen paraded herself before me. I noticed that she wore the blouse without a

23

bra underneath, and her breasts and nipples showed clearly through the flimsy material.

'You're not going to go around like that, are you?' I said.

'Why not? This is the age of permissive enlightenment, isn't it?'

'Hmm. . . .'

I noticed, though, that the following week, when the first guests arrived she, like all the other girls, wore a bra. Maybe there was as much bluff about Doreen as I had first guessed.

That first week with guests, I saw the camp coming to life around me. I was desperately busy, not so much because of the number of guests (this early in the season the camp was only half full) but because I was still unfamiliar with the routines. By the second week I was more into the swing of things, and by the third week – which was the first one in which the camp was fully-booked – I was feeling at home both with the work and the people. I saw less of Doreen as we worked harder.

I was friendly with several of the other girls, but we were all working different shifts and I found myself on my own more often than not. It was not surprising, therefore, that I turned to the guests for my social life.

We girls (we were known officially as 'stewardettes') had the full run of the camp and its facilities during our off-duty hours. I found that I was living it up as I had never done before . . . drinking in the bars to the early hours of the morning, or dancing in the camp discotheque or night-club.

My wages went straight into my Post Office book every week. Apart from a few shillings spent on tights, make-up and cigarettes there was really nothing to spend money on at all.

I was offered more drinks than I could accept, and when I worked the late shift behind one of the bars I made enough in tips to see me through all incidental expenses.

It was in short a really enjoyable life.

Quite a few men danced with me and tried to date me, but I was determined not to get involved. Not for me one of those two-week holiday romances. Apart from the occasional man I allowed to escort me back to shanty-town, and the quick peck goodnight, my sex-life was nil. What was more, I wasn't missing it.

It wasn't until I met Paul that this rosy picture changed. I should have known that a small part of me was still hooked on the memory of my ex-'fiance'. The fact that this second Paul shared the name, had the same fair hair and grey eyes was enough to

24

stir the old body chemistry into action.

We met, you might say, in the course of business.

I was on waitress duty in the restaurant. It was a busy day, and I was not on my best form. I think I'd had a few too many vodka and limes the night before.

I'm still not quite sure what happened. One minute I was traipsing along with a bowl of hot soup that some guest had wanted returned to the kitchen, and the next I was gazing in horror at a warm, steaming and brown-windsor coloured patch in this young man's lap.

Whether I tripped, or whether he had deliberately engineered some kind of accident I shall never know. If he did engineer it, then it must have been some masochistic streak in him, for he certainly howled with pain when the sticky fluid hit him.

I gaped in panic at the damage.

'I'm . . . sorry!' I burbled, wishing to God everyone would stop staring at me.

He said nothing, but pushed back his chair slightly, and tried to hold the material away from his skin. He was wearing a pair of light-blue slacks which were most obviously ruined.

I knelt down in front of him, and in desperation began dabbing at the stain with my cloth.

He returned from his state of anguish to one of calmness. He watched me as I mopped away, grinning slightly.

In my haste to clean up, I dabbed frantically at the wet patch, not fully realising exactly where I was devoting my attentions.

He leaned forward slightly, so that his face came close to my ear.

'You've got rather a nice touch. Care to try it out sometime where it's a bit less public?'

Still not getting the message, I suddenly noticed with some alarm the very considerable bulge in the vicinity of the stain. At once, I was overcome with a confusion which made my previous state seem like one of tranquil calm. I blushed furiously, stood up abruptly, and beat a hasty retreat. I felt fifty pairs of eyes following me as I ran from the restaurant.

Fortunately, word couldn't have got back to the management, for I never heard a word of reprimand about the accident.

But the incident wasn't closed.

That evening I was in the night-club. I had been helping one of the male organisers run a spot-prize for a dance, and was relaxing over a gin and tonic at the bar. Then the young man walked up to me.

'Hello there,' he said. 'Can I buy you a drink?'

I looked at him coldly. Not because I felt cold towards him, but it was a way of concealing the embarrassment I still felt.

'No thank you.'

'Come on, now. I only want to show there are no hard feelings. My name's Paul. What's yours?'

'Sally,' I said, before I could stop myself.

'Good. Then we're old friends. Or at least, that's the impression I got from your eagerness this morning.'

I looked at him, seeing his face wreathed in a friendly smile. It was no good, I couldn't resist him. I laughed, and let him buy me another gin.

We stood there for about half an hour, chatting amiably. After a couple of drinks, he led me out on to the dance floor, and we smooched around. It might have been the music, it might have been the drink . . . it might have been his persuasive manner. But in very few minutes I was feeling sleepy and happy. Paul's body was pressed up to mine, and slowly I became aware of a certain male object pressing hard against me, making like an athlete in the prime of life.

Paul put his mouth to my ear.

'I'm afraid I'm not going to be able to make love to you tonight. Oscar got rather badly scalded this morning.'

Quite apart from the manifest lie – 'Oscar' was obviously in fighting form – I was appalled by the arrogance of him. I was just making up my mind whether to slap his face or run from the dance-floor, when he grabbed hold of my wrist and rubbed my hand up against his crutch.

'Here, say sorry to him.'

I tried to raise my hand to slap him, but he held my wrist in a vice-like grip.

'Before you do anything silly,' Paul murmured, 'just remember that we are on a crowded dance-floor, that I am a guest and that you work here. Knocking the customers around might not please the management.'

I was furious. It took all my will-power to stop myself from bringing my knee up into his groin.

I twisted free and almost ran out of the club.

Once outside, I lit a cigarette to calm myself and stood for a moment in the dark, trembling with rage. After a few drags on the cigarette, I walked away quickly, up the hill towards shanty-town.

There were no lights on in the dormitory-hut.

I walked in. As I opened the door I heard a squeaking symphony of bedsprings coming to a sudden halt.

A female voice called out nervously.

'Who's that?'

I recognised Doreen's voice at once.

'It's only me, Doreen,' I said, and fumbled for the light-switch by the door.

'Don't put the light on, there's a love,' Doreen said urgently. I heard movements from her bed . . . a rustle of sheets, springs creaking slightly. 'Sally, I don't suppose you could sort of stroll around the camp for quarter of an hour, could you?'

I was slow catching on; still preoccupied with my anger about Paul.

'I beg your pardon?' I said.

'You heard her,' said a male voice. 'Scram!'

Suddenly I got the message, and backed towards the door.

'Sorry,' I mumbled, and let myself out. The bedsprings started up their song once more, and I heard Doreen throw in a few moans and groans of pleasure for good measure.

It was the first sign I had that she was more than halfway serious about what she had told me.

Thoroughly depressed now, I walked back through the darkened camp towards the lights and noise of the central complex of buildings.

'Can a man say he's sorry?'

I nearly jumped out of my skin. I whirled round, and saw Paul standing a few yards behind me. He had been waiting for me beside a lighted notice-board, and in the dim glow from the lamp I could see the expression on his face. It was totally different from the last time I had seen him, only a few minutes before.

'If you come one step closer,' I said, 'I shall scream.' Believe me, I meant it. I quickened my pace, and headed for the nearest building.

Paul followed quickly. He ran in front of me, and blocked my path.

'Look . . . I really am sorry. I got carried away. You just turn me on, and I'm sorry.'

I glared at him, and saw that he appeared to mean it. I saw him then as I had seen him earlier, in the bar of the night-club. He smiled at me, hopefully, and spread his arms wide in a helpless gesture. It was just too much. He could have charmed me to death with a smile on my face. All my tensions rose to the surface and bubbled over in a mixture of laughter and tears.

I wasn't really listening as Paul burst into a torrent of renewed apologies. We walked together through the almost-deserted chalet-area, round the swimming-pool and past the ballroom, where strains of 'Anniversary Waltz' came drifting through the open door.

In a few minutes we were past the central area, and back in the seemingly endless rows of chalets.

'Coming in for a coffee?' he asked suddenly, stopping outside one of the chalets.

And that was the strange thing. As Paul spoke, a series of mental pictures flashed through my mind. Paul was undoubtedly an expert seducer, even though his methods were as crude and unsubtle as could be imagined. I saw myself going into the chalet, I saw Paul jumping on me with little or no pretence, I saw him calmly and methodically removing my clothes and sliding me into his bed.

I saw all this; realised exactly what would happen . . . but I still accepted his offer.

I didn't see it at the time, but the basic fallacy of the idea of a holiday camp being a world in isolation was beginning to reach me.

I followed Paul into the chalet, just like the proverbial fly into the spider's parlour. As things turned out, my predictions were wrong in only one sense: Paul didn't take my clothes off.

He was starting to strip almost as soon as I closed the door.

'You don't want coffee any more than I do,' he said calmly. 'It only keeps you awake at night.'

Without so much as touching me, he finished undressing and climbed into the double bed. There was absolutely nothing to prevent me turning on my heel, walking out of the chalet and closing the door behind me.

But I didn't. Paul's magnetic attraction for me must have been stronger than I knew. I slipped off my blouse and mini-skirt, and fumbled with the clasp of my bra. He reached out lazily from the bed and closed his hand around my knee, sliding it slowly upwards. His fingers seemed to probe gently at my flesh wherever he touched, as though he were testing it for firmness, smoothness and general texture.

I dropped my bra, and slid my fingers into the band of my panties. I had to step back a little from him, to release myself from his grasp, then stepped out of the filmy material. I stood naked before him, and regarded him. Some men appear to be born for sex, and Paul was one of them. I guessed that love-

28

making came naturally to him ... so naturally that it meant nothing to him except as a sequence of actions which were conducted with the maximum of skill and technique. Perhaps also he expected everyone else to be as calm and objective as he. I suspected he was a taker of a pleasure ... not a giver. Nevertheless, I was prepared to allow him to take his pleasures. I was not acting consciously; merely following some inner guide which prevented me from doing anything but stand here before him, my body revealed to his gaze.

His hand continued its passage up my thighs, reaching through my legs and caressing the muscle at the back of my right leg. Up and up it went, until it rested firmly on my buttocks, kneading the flesh.

Gently, I was propelled forward to the side of his bed, and then with his other hand he flipped back the covers. I saw at once that he was aroused. I moved towards him, lying down beside him.

Paul's lips brushed across mine in a fleeting kiss ... the first and last time he ever kissed me.

On the mouth.

Now his hands seemed to be everywhere about my body, and in a moment he ducked beneath the covers and followed his hands with his mouth. I felt his fingers, and then his tongue, slip expertly across my breasts, teasing the nipples, then on down, across my belly, and then on further down . . . .

His movements were very slow, very calm and very deliberate. The sensation was indescribable: I felt in me a slowly mounting heat that I knew only one thing could cool. For what seemed like hours, his hands and mouth worked their way across my body, finding places of arousal on my skin that I had hardly suspected existed.

I could feel myself straining towards him like I had never done with any man before. I was desperately tired of his game, raised to such a fever-pitch of excitement that I wanted him to stop his teasing and thrust himself into me.

Then suddenly he stopped, and his grinning face re-appeared from beneath the sheets.

'Sorry, dear,' he said off-handedly. 'Don't think I'm going to be able to make it tonight.'

I was literally gasping with desire.

'You bastard!' I screamed. It was partly a genuine curse, and partly a line which seemed to generate spontaneously, as if I knew it was what he wanted me to say.

29

It seemed to excite him. He thrashed around in the bed, kicking at the bedclothes and hurling them on to the floor. He threw himself on to me with a powerful surge of his lithe young body, his hands probing gently at the moistness between my thighs. With his knees, he prised my legs apart, and struggled into position. Then . . . about a century too late for my liking, he entered me.

The next few minutes were almost agonising in their sheer sensual pleasure. I lost count of the number of times I felt myself lifted up on the surging wave of orgasm, only to plunge into a trough of warm sweat and liquid fatigue. Paul came once, rested for a moment, and then without unlinking began those unique movements once more. Several times, I nearly cried out that I could not take any more ecstasy.

Then, with one final shuddering orgasm, we both dived together into that trough of pleasurable fatigue, and it was all over.

I lay on my back struggling for breath, then gasped as I felt Paul's body withdraw itself from me. He slumped beside me, his hand resting on one of my breasts.

Five minutes later, I was nearly asleep, drifting away.

Paul murmured: 'Tomorrow I think we shall experiment with a few of the minor perversions.'

I was too sleepy to register any reaction.

I awoke to a loud and repetitive banging on the door of the chalet. The sunlight was streaming in through the tiny window, and I caught a glimpse of Paul's bedside clock. It was ten past seven.

'My God!' I said, waking Paul. 'I'm supposed to be on duty!'

He heard the knocking at the door.

'Who is it?' he said, sleepily.

'Chalet bed service,' came the reply, and I recognised the voice as belonging to Betty, one of the girls in my dormitory-hut.

I looked at Paul in panic.

'Don't let her in,' I said softly. 'It's one of the girls from my dormitory. If she sees me here, it will be all round the camp by afternoon.'

'OK,' Paul said, grinning. 'I'll preserve your virginal reputation.'

He climbed out of bed, and padded naked across the floor to the door.

'What are you doing?' I hissed.

'You'll see.'

He opened the door unashamedly, holding it wide so that the

girl would have no doubts as to his state of undress.

'Would you mind terribly if you came back later?' he said in an exaggerated public-school accent.

I couldn't see Betty's reaction from the bed – the open door intervened, fortunately – but I heard her let out a half-strangled scream, and then she hurried away.

Paul closed the door, and came purposefully towards me. He was fully awake, in more senses than one, and I understood why Betty had screamed.

'Now for my favourite breakfast,' he said.

'Oh no you don't,' I said, and rolled off the bed. 'I'm already late for work.'

I found my clothes in a crumpled heap on the floor, and pulled them on frantically. Paul jumped back into bed, and pulled the sheets over him.

I opened the chalet-door, and peered out cautiously. There was no one in sight. Betty must have gone into one of the other chalets.

'I'll see you later,' I heard Paul say from the bed.

'Maybe,' I replied, and went outside, slamming the door behind me.

I hurried off towards shanty-town.

CHAPTER 3

THE dormitory was deserted. I ran inside, and tore off my clothes. They were terribly creased and crumpled, and I couldn't possibly wear them for work. I had a spare blouse, but only the one skirt. I found the iron we shared, and switched it on. While it was warming up, I dived into the shower.

Afterwards, I slipped on clean underwear, found the spare blouse and hurriedly pressed the skirt. Then I ran down to the central complex of buildings.

It was too late to report to the staff office, so I went instead straight to the restaurant where I knew I was on breakfast duties.

Just outside the staff entrance I bumped into Alan Spiers.

'Ah ... it's Sally, isn't it?'

'Yes.'

31

'Overslept, I take it?'

'That's right.'

He frowned.

'Funny how the other girls in your dormitory let you sleep in. They're usually very keen to see no one gets more than their fair share of sleep.'

I knew what he meant. In a roomful of girls it was impossible to oversleep.

'Never mind. I'm not going ro reprimand you for it. We all make mistakes.' I assumed that was the end of it, and made to move on but he reached out and held me by the arm. 'I saw you last night, Sally. In the night club. You seemed to be very friendly with one of the guests.'

'That's my business,' I said, sullenly.

'Yes . . . but it's our business too. They're our customers you know. I hate to say this, Sally, but you must be more careful. The management are not keen on seeing affairs between staff and guests.'

'It was nothing. There's nothing going on.'

He nodded.

'If you say so.' His expression changed, and I felt the grip on my arm ease a little. 'Look, Sally, the next time you feel yourself becoming – ah – involved with one of the guests, why not drop in to see me?'

I stared at him. What did he mean? His tone was still harsh, as though he were reprimanding me in spite of his denial that he was . . . and yet, the touch of his hand on my arm was almost gentle. He had the fingers of his hand inside, so that they lightly touched the edge of my breast. Was that deliberate? It was so hard to tell.

'I can look after myself, thanks all the same.' I was keeping my voice even, not being falsely friendly, and not being cold either.

'OK. Have it your way. But listen, come to my office after you've finished the breakfast shift.'

'Is that a request or an order?'

' I think. . . .' He was looking at me with his eyes narrowed. 'I think, that as you want to make the differentiation, that is it an order.'

I pulled my arm free.

'All right, Mister Spiers. I'll come.'

'Good.' He turned on his heel, and strode away from me.

Wow. The electricity had fairly sparked. What was it between us that caused such a high-voltage discharge?

In the restaurant-kitchen, Doreen winked at me.

'Hi.'

'Hi.'

'Sorry about last night. I didn't know anyone'd be coming back.'

'I'm sorry too, Doreen. I should have realised sooner.'

'Good. No damage done then.'

We put on the white caps we wore when we were serving, and dashed out through the swing doors to administer to the needs of hungry campers. Fruit juice or corn-flakes. Kippers or bacon. Toast and marmalade. And a nice pot of tea.

The session went comparatively smoothly. The only complication was that I saw Paul had somehow wangled his way on to a table in my section of the restaurant. He smiled broadly at me, and I nodded back.

I took orders from all the tables except the one he was on, then ducked into the kitchen.

'Daph!' I called to one of the girls as she was on her way back to the restaurant. 'Do us a favour? I've got a personal problem on Table 17. Do that one for me, and I'll do one of yours extra this evening.'

She grinned understandingly, and carried on her way.

When the breakfast was over, and the announcements of the day were called out (Men vs. Women on the football field, relay races in the swimming-pool, and the third round of the table-tennis championship in the sports room) I went with the other girls for our own breakfast.

Then, with certain misgivings, I went to see Alan Spiers.

I knocked timidly on the door of his office. There was a long pause.

Then: 'Come in.'

I walked in. Alan looked up, and nodded towards a chair on the other side of his desk.

I sat down.

'I've got your cards ready if you want them,' he said.

'So I'm being sacked, am I?' I should have guessed it would be something of the sort.

'You're putting words into my mouth. I said they're ready for you if you want them.'

'And if I don't?'

Alan smiled . . . the first trace of humour that day.

'Then I'll put them back in the cabinet. Look here, Sally, I think we ought to have a serious talk.'

'OK. That's what I came here for.'

He shuffled uneasily with a paper-knife, and I found myself looking at him in a way I had not done before. I suddenly realised what it was about him that made me uneasy: he was too young-looking for the job. A manager of personnel should be middle-aged, a kind of uncle-figure. Alan Spiers looked more like a well-fed and retired pop-singer than someone who looked after fifty-odd staff.

'Sally, to me it seems obvious that this is the first time you've been in a holiday camp, either as a guest or as an employee. Am I right?'

I shook my head.

'Not quite. I came here, to this camp, when I was a child.'

'Ah yes . . . you said something about that once before. But I take it you haven't been to one since?'

'That's right.'

'OK then. In which case it's about time you and I got a few things clear. First of all, I'm not even sure quite how to talk to you. You're not like most of the other girls. You're younger for a start, and – how can I put this? – rather less worldly. I'm used to dealing with the real hard nuts . . . the professionals and the scrubbers who are usually attracted to this place.' He paused, looking at me thoughtfully. 'You know what I mean?'

I thought of Doreen, and her bravura talking.

'Yes, I know what you mean,' I said.

Alan looked relieved, as if he hadn't wanted to explain in painstaking detail.

'Now I'm going to make a few suppositions,' he continued, 'and you can correct me if I'm wrong. First of all, it's my guess that you're only here because you were trying to escape from something . . . right?'

'Right. You're very perceptive. Unfortunately, I was the wrong sex for the French Foreign Legion.'

'It's my job to perceive,' he said. 'I wouldn't be much of a personnel manager if I couldn't sum up people and their problems. Anyway, what I wanted to say was this: if that was what you wanted, then you can start to relax a bit. Just take it easy and make the most of the few months you have in this place. Because if it is escape you're after, then you've found it. In fact, you've found one of the best places in the world.'

'I thought –' I started to say, but Alan was in full spate.

'The minute you walk through the main gate into the camp,

34

you're in a new, almost foreign country. It's not real. It's a carefully and deliberately constructed dream; planned, designed, pre-packed and polythene wrapped as an existence with the sole function of providing escape.

'Now the guests only get a couple of weeks of it at the most ... but while they are in here they live in that different world and they make the most of it. They leave their jobs and their problems and their bills outside that gate, and they don't worry about them until they walk out again. You're better off than the guests, Sally ... you have several months of it to look forward to.

'The best way I can put it is this: just try to imagine you are in a completely different country where none of the old rules apply. You won't go far wrong.'

'Why are you telling me all this?' I said. I understood everything he told me, but didn't see how it applied to me.

'Because you of all the girls here seem to be making the least of it. I haven't been watching you – don't think that – but whenever I've seen you, you've always appeared to have all the troubles in the world on your shoulder. This is a holiday-camp, Sally ... accent on "holiday". People are here to enjoy themselves, and if you're marching around the camp with a black expression, it doesn't do our image all that good.'

So it was a company line he was feeding me.

'I'm ... sorry, Alan. I hadn't realised I gave that impression.'

'Sally, *is* there anything you don't like about the camp?'

'No.'

'I mean really. You can speak in confidence.'

I paused.

'Only ... I'm not sure.' I glanced at him. He was waiting patiently, and I thought it would do no harm to confide in him. 'There is something, Alan. It's the other girls. They seem to expect me to ... behave like they do.'

He nodded slowly.

'You mean, working the racket?'

'So you know about it.'

'Of course. I wasn't born yesterday. No, there's no way of stopping them if that's what they want to do ... unofficially of course. Strictly speaking, they would be sacked if they were ever caught ... but they're pretty careful. And what would happen if we sacked them? We'd have to hire more girls, and in time the new lot would be doing the same. All I can do is turn a blind eye, and make sure that no one's high principles are offended. By and large, what goes on is very discreet, and I doubt if many people are even aware of it. On the face of it, this is a nice, respectable family camp . . . and that's the image we strive to maintain at all costs. Of course, we get single men coming here looking for a good time, and that's what some of the girls exploit. What am I to do? Instigate a reign of terror? All that would do is drive it more underground.'

'So what am I to do?'

Alan grinned at me.

'That's up to you Sally. I can't offer any better advice than that. If you don't like it, you may have your cards and go. That's why I had them ready for you. But I'd be sorry to see you go. You're not alone in your distaste for this. You don't *have* to be involved. I think that in general it's a good life here. The work's hard, but it's enjoyable.'

I bit my lower lip.

'Can you tell me . . . what's the company's attitude towards affairs between guests and staff?'

'You mean that man in the club last night?'

'You were there?'

Alan nodded slowly.

'I guessed something was going on. There's no problem there, apart from your own feelings. Just be careful and discreet.'

I said: 'There's nothing going on. He was just chatting me up, that's all.'

'Then there's no problem. As I said.'

He stared at me thoughtfully, drumming the tips of his fingers against the table-top. I found myself desperately wanting a cigarette, and wished he'd offer me one. He said no more, and eventually I realised that the interview was over.

I stood up, awkwardly.

'Thanks, Alan. I do appreciate your trying to help.'

'Forget it. Go on, make the most of your off-time before the lunch-hour rush.'

I nodded, and walked out of his office in a very thoughtful frame of mind. I felt that although Alan had not said anything that referred completely and specifically to me, what he had said helped me put the whole business of life and work in the camp into perspective.

I didn't want to laze around and get too introverted, so I thought I'd go and help out with the table-tennis competition. They were always short of staff on those functions and Mac – the Scottish games supervisor – welcomed me thankfully. He gave me a brief rundown of the rules, then dashed off to the swimming-pool to see how the relay-races were getting on.

I didn't know the first thing about table-tennis, but believe me I soon learned. For me, the most amusing match was between a very uptight-looking young man of about 24 – who was kitted out with about five different bats – and a very weedy schoolboy. The table-tennis champ obviously thought he was going to walk it, and dazzled us all with his first few flashy shots. But after a few services, the boy found his length and soon had no difficulty in wiping the young man around the floor.

As I scribbled the kid's name on the blackboard, I rewarded him with my most devastating smile. You could almost feel the happiness radiating from him.

After this, I still had half-an-hour to kill before lunch, and soon I found myself strolling towards Paul's chalet.

I knocked on the door, and he answered. He was wearing very brief bathing-trunks, and his hair was tousled and wet.

'You find me in my hour of glory,' he said. 'Men's relay-champion to be . . . you wait. We knocked hell out of them, and now we're in the final.'

'If you're busy . . .' I said.

'No . . . come on in. I'm just changing for lunch.' He grabbed me by the hand. 'I thought you'd never get here.'

'What do you mean?' I said. 'I made no arrangement to call.'

'Ah, but I knew you wouldn't be able to stay away for long. Come on, get your clothes off. We've just got time for a quick one before lunch.'

I pulled away from him. After the sympathetic attentions of Alan that morning, Paul's arrogance was quite repulsive.

'Please, Paul,' I said. 'I came here for a quiet chat, that's all.'

I don't think Paul was listening. He reached forward and started to unbutton my blouse.

'What you really want, my girl, is what all women want. Well, you've come to the right place at the right time.'

I pulled away again, angrily.

'You crude bastard,' I shouted. 'Have you nothing else in that tiny little mind of yours?'

'I didn't think it was my mind that interested you.' he said nastily. He grabbed me, and threw me forcibly on to the bed. As I struggled to climb up, he pushed down his trunks and moved towards me. 'There you are. All yours. Just squeeze a little, and modern miracles will abound.'

I managed to wriggle away from under him, and got to my feet. He seized my sleeve, ripping the cloth around one of the buttons at the front. Paul collapsed on the bed, laughing.

I opened the chalet door.

'Don't worry, Sally. I'm not that keen on it myself at this time of day. Come back when you're ready for it, but don't expect me to save you a place in the queue.'

I slammed the door with all the force I could muster, and ran through the chalets, hurriedly doing up the buttons of my blouse. The one that was torn was at the front, between my breasts. As the material strained, a patch of my white bra could be glimpsed underneath . . . but it was nothing to worry about. It looked quite like an ordinary tear.

But Paul! My God, the sheer gall of the man!

I ran until I came to the children's boating-lake, and realised that I had never had that cigarette. I sat down by myself in a quiet corner, and smoked earnestly and with great concentration until I felt calmer. I forced myself not to think about Paul, and turned instead to Alan.

Though he'd made no special appeal to me on a personal level, the idea of seeing him as an alternative to Paul was irresistible. It was the first time the thought had crossed my mind, but in truth Alan was really quite attractive and desirable. Until this morning he had been simply a boss . . . but in the light of our private interview, I felt that he had taken more than a usual interest in my personality and identity. Alan had been until then simply a boss, but now I found myself thinking about him as a man.

I let the thoughts run away with themselves, and I indulged myself in a harmless fantasy, where it was Alan and not Paul who had made love to me during the night. . . .

'Steady on, Sal,' I said grimly. 'Mustn't mix business with pleasure. There's probably some company rule about not falling in love with other members of the staff.'

They say that a cold bath is a good cure for over-erotic thoughts, so I decided to have a quick swim before lunch. I was halfway across towards shanty-town to collect my bikini, when I heard the lunch-gong being broadcast over the P.A.

'Damn!' I muttered. I'd lost all sense of time. For the second time that day, I hurried with more speed than grace to the restaurant.

Preoccupied as I was, I managed to get through that session without any accidents, then went with the others to the staff canteen for my own lunch.

In the afternoon, I was on duty in the children's nursery. This was probably one of the most energetic jobs on the camp, but one I always found rather relaxing. I like children, and although several were as rowdy as all hell I enjoyed myself. I was doing things without thinking . . . and that suited me fine.

By five o'clock I was exhausted, but far calmer inside. Officially, I then had another hour's break before dinner, but I got involved with Jimmy, the social organiser, who wanted a hand sorting out the spot-prizes for the dance that evening. Halfway through the work I saw that it was time for me go to on duty in the restaurant once more, but Jimmy saw how tired I was.

'Do you want to cut the restaurant tonight?'

I nodded gratefully.

'I'll see what I can do,' he said.

He was gone about three minutes. 'Finish off in here with me, and you can have the rest of the evening off.'

'How did you wangle that?'

'Oh . . . I saw Alan outside. He said it'd be OK.'

'Phew . . . that's a relief. It's been a long day.'

We pumped up about a dozen more balloons, and got them into the net. Then I helped Jimmy winch it up to the ceiling, from where they'd be released at the appropriate moment.

'That's OK, Sally. You go and have a rest. I can finish off.'

I smiled at him with frank gratitude, and dragged my heels up through the camp towards shanty-town.

I went into the dormitory, and collapsed backwards on to the bed. I could almost see the steam rising from my poor, tired feet. I was still lying there, exactly as I had fallen, when Doreen came in half an hour later.

'Hello, love. You look knocked out.'

'I bloody well feel it, too,' I said, levering myself into a sitting position.

'Fancy going down to one of the bars and having a drink?' Doreen asked, sitting on her own bed, and kicking off her shoes. 'I've got a date at 10, but nothing much to do in the meantime.'

'Well . . . I'm a bit tired,' I said hesitantly. 'Your date tonight – is he a paying customer?'

'Of course, love. I never give it away for free these days. The season's just getting going.'

'OK, we'll have a drink then,' I said. 'But don't expect me to play along with you if you want to pick up a couple of potential customers. There's plenty of time for you before 10 o'clock.'

Doreen grinned. It was absolutely impossible to get past her, or even get sarcasm through her hide.

'Don't worry, Sally. We had this out once, and I know you're straight. Anyway, my mark tonight will be paying double prices. He's a 'speciality' case.'

I got the feeling that Doreen was about to describe how she catered to this 'speciality', so I quickly changed the subject.

'Alan Spiers called me into his office today.'

'Oh? A ticking-off?'

'That's what I thought it was going to be at first. No, it was just a friendly heart-to-heart chat.'

'Lucky you,' said Doreen. 'Give me ten minutes alone with him, and I'd have his trousers off . . . despite what everyone says.'

'What do you mean by that?'

'Well you know that everyone thinks he's bent, don't you? He jokes and messes around with the girls, but he's never made any really serious attempt at anyone.'

I felt impelled to stick up for Alan under this attack, which I considered to be very unfair.

'That doesn't mean he has to be queer,' I said. 'Perhaps he just doesn't want to become involved with other members of the staff. He's in a dodgy position, you know . . . halfway between the staff and the guests.'

Doreen didn't convince easily.

'Come off it, Sally. Whoever heard of a normal bloke turning down the chance of a bit on the side? Let's face it, Alan could have just about any of the girls he fancied. I mean, he's a marvellous looking feller.'

Time for another change of subject. I stood up, and began to unbutton my blouse. I looked round for a dress to put on.

'Come on, Doreen. How about that drink then?'

CHAPTER 4

AFTER a couple of vodka and limes I was feeling more lively. After the third, I was positively sparkling. And yet, I was as nothing beside Doreen. She drank two to my every one, and didn't seem to change in the slightest. When she got around to buying me my fourth, and her seventh, I thought it was time to cool it.

'Well,' I said. 'I think I'll go to bed.'

Doreen looked a little alarmed.

'Aren't you sleeping out tonight, then?'

'No I'm not. Why?'

'Oh dear.' She sighed. 'Then it's a bit awkward.'

'You mean, you . . .'

She nodded.

'I'm sorry, Sally. I'd assumed you would be kipping with your bloke again tonight. My mark is coming round to Shanty-town tonight . . . because I can't go to his chalet. His wife's there. I've got it organised with the other girls. They won't be in until much later.'

'Oh, that's just great,' I said angrily. 'That's bloody marvellous.'

'I'm sorry, love,' she said again. 'I didn't know.'

Doreen fell silent, and bought herself another vodka. She swilled it around in the glass for a while, then appeared to brighten.

'I've got an idea,' she said. 'Why don't you go back now, go to bed and just keep quiet when we come in? I'll make sure not to put the lights on, so the mark won't see you, and you probably won't even wake up. If you do, just keep quiet while I deliver the goods. It won't take long.'

I pondered on this for a while. Unpleasant though it sounded, I couldn't think of any alternative. Short of going to find Paul . . . and that was out of the question.

'I don't really have much choice, do I? But I'll tell you what . . . get me another drink before I go, and make it a double. It'll help me sleep.'

'It's a deal.' Doreen walked over to the bar, and came back a moment later with the drink. I tipped it up, and swallowed it in two mouthfuls.

'Right,' I said, and stood up. 'I'm off.'

I sat down again in a hurry. Why hadn't they built this bar with a level floor? From my point of view, it was going up and down like the North Atlantic in a Force 10 gale.

Doreen helped me to the door. She didn't exactly carry me, but walked at my side gripping my arm.

'Can you make it back to shanty-town?'

'Leave it to me,' I slurred. 'Just point me in the right direction.'

I staggered off, leaving Doreen with a worried frown. Though the night air helped a little, I was still incredibly drunk. Fortunately, I met no one on the way whom I recognised, and a few minutes later found myself leaning on the door of the dormitory, trying to find the handle. Someone thoughtless appeared to have moved it to another part of the door . . . but when I eventually found it, it still worked and I lurched inside.

I went to the loo, then undressed and fell into bed without bothering to put on my nightie.

I waited for sleep to overtake me.

For some strange reason, the walls, floor and ceiling were whizzing round me in ever-decreasing circles. In a moment of drunken concentration, I found myself speculating whether Priest's Cave Holiday Centre was built on an earthquake zone, and if so was I at the epicentre. The whizzing had a kind of fascination of its own, and after a while I stopped worrying about it.

Sleep still seemed to be a stubbornly long way away. For a while I felt as if I were falling into a deep pit, but then I jolted awake again.

I was still fully conscious when I heard the door-handle rattle quietly. It was Doreen and her 'mark'.

I lay with my eyes closed, determined not to move.

I heard them whispering quietly, and detected the soft rustle of clothes as they undressed. Then came that unmistakable sound of bed-springs as they climbed into the bed next to mine.

I'll say one thing for Doreen: she didn't waste any time in getting down to business. Almost at once she began her grunting and moaning, interspersed with the occasional sound of heavy breathing from her friend.

The noises in the background continued, but I became aware of heavy breathing much closer. I tried to locate it, then discovered much to my surprise that it was emanating from myself. Without even being conscious of it I had become sexually aroused. I investigated at once, and found that my thighs were moist, my nipples erect.

Somehow it seemed to me that Doreen's bed and mine had joined together to make one, and that the coupling couple were lying in the sheets next to me. I began to wish above everything else that this nameless man would reach out, would touch my breasts, press his face into my tenderness, would thrust himself into me. Unconsciously, I reached out in their direction, and sure enough they were lying there.

The man came to me, pressing his lips to mine. I reached up, traced the contours of his face with my hand. I knew those features. . . .

It was Paul!

I couldn't stop him now . . . his hands and mouth were roaming all over my body. I cried out for him to stop, but it only made his efforts the greater.

I fell silent, listening again to the sounds from Doreen. Paul was quiet too, touching me, but not speaking.

Then I recognised what Doreen was hissing through partly-opened lips.

'KissmeAlan . . . kissmeAlan . . . kissmeAlan. . . .'

Her mark was Alan Spiers!

I felt Paul working himself into position, forcing apart my legs. I didn't want him . . . I wanted Alan. Brutally, I thrust him aside, and leaped from the bed.

I ran to the wall by the door, fumbled for the light-switch.

The whole length of the dormitory, the lights came on. I blinked in the sudden brightness.

'Doreen! How could you!'

And I looked . . . and I saw that her bed was empty. . . .

The only disturbed bed was mine, and on that the sheets had been thrashed into an untidy heap.

It had all been an erotic dream.

It took me several seconds to re-acclimatise myself to the reality. The alcohol was still fuddling my brain, and the dream and the reality mixed in a confusing melange of impressions.

Only one thing was totally real to me . . . the fact that I was in a state of almost insatiable sexual arousal. I tried to fight it, but it only grew worse. It had to be sated, and I knew only one man I wanted who would satisfy me.

Alan Spiers.

My whole body yearned for him. I loved him and I desired him, and I wanted only one thing in life. Immediate sexual union with him. And yet he was unattainable.

I knew it was the drink, and I knew I could do nothing about it. But I was not capable of being sensible. I wanted Alan, and I wanted him now.

I walked back unsteadily to my bedside. I found my light, nylon dressing-gown, and pulled it over my naked body.

I switched off the lights in the dormitory, and staggered out into the night.

The air was cool, and I let the dressing-gown hang open, so that the air bathed over my body.

Alan. . . .

How could I find him?

Blindly, I walked through the dark towards the centre of the camp.

'Sally? Is that you?'

I turned round quickly, and nearly over-balanced.

'Who is it?'

'It's me . . . Paul. I wanted to say how sorry I was . . .'

I closed my eyes. I didn't want Paul.

'Hey, you've got no clothes on. Where are you going? I came up here looking for you, because you weren't in the bar.'

I said indistinctly: 'Are you Alan?'

'Pardon?'

'Are you Alan?'

'Yeah, yeah. I'm Alan.' He must have detected my drunken state; he could have hardly mistaken it. 'Come on. I'll take you to my chalet. It isn't far.'

He came over to me, and I tried to step away. I stumbled, and he caught me, scooping me up into his arms.

'I like you drunk, Sally. I like you like this.'

'Put me down . . .' I tried to say, but he wasn't listening. I felt my dressing gown hanging down, so that to all intents and purposes I was naked in his arms. I felt cold, but it did not matter. I closed my eyes, imagined that he was Alan.

I was hardly aware of our arrival at his chalet, but came to as he laid me on his bed, and pulled the dressing-gown from my shoulders. He took off his clothes, and I looked at his magnificent naked body . . . but saw what I wanted to see of his face.

His face was not Paul's.

And then he was in bed beside me, and I felt my arousal renewing. But it was not for Paul that I warmed, not for Paul's body that my thighs moistened . . . .

CHAPTER 5

WHEN morning came I had a mouth like the Kalahari Desert, and a head like a bucketful of pebbles. My first awareness was of Paul moving . . . and of course by that time I had no doubt in my mind who he really was.

Paul was standing in front of his mirror shaving as I managed to lift myself into a sitting position.

'God, that razor's got a loud motor.'

He turned round. His face was covered with shaving cream, and he held a Gillette safety-razor in his right hand.

'Motor? What motor?'

I stared at him.

'Sorry. It must be coming from inside.'

He finished shaving, then washed noisily in the sink.

'What's the time?'

'Half past eight.'

I'd missed the morning shift . . . and frankly I couldn't have cared less. All I wanted to do was sleep.

'Well . . . I'm off to have one of the delicious breakfasts they serve here. You coming?'

'Like this? Without any clothes? You've got to be joking.'

Then I gulped silently to myself. I was a virtual prisoner in his chalet. The only garment I had was the dressing-gown, and that was almost transparent. It was one thing to walk around in it late at night, pissed out of my mind, but it was something else again to walk through the camp in broad daylight like it.

I pointed out the salient facts to Paul.

He laughed, and at first I thought he was going to exploit my helplessness.

'Don't worry. I'll see what I can fix for you. Who can I get to find some clothes for you?'

'Do you know Doreen? The very tall girl, with the good figure. She's my friend. If you can find her, she'll get some clothes for me.'

'OK. Wait here.'

It was the only thing he ever did for me that was motivated out of the tiny bit of goodness in his heart. I had a quick snooze while he was gone, and woke up when he returned.

'Here.' He threw a bundle of my clothes to me. 'All decent again.'

'Thanks, Paul.'

I got out of bed hastily, and began to pull them on.

'There's no hurry, you know. Doreen said she'd get one of the others to do your shift for you, provided you return the favour later on.'

I nodded. I just wanted to get out of that chalet as soon as possible.

'You coming to see me tonight?' Paul went on. 'Tonight being what it is?'

'What is it? Just a Friday.'

'Yes . . . and tomorrow's Saturday. The day when I pack up and return to my wife and seventeen kids. And the day when a brand-new batch of happy holidaymakers crowd in.'

'It'll be nice to see some new faces,' I said, adding to myself that it'd also be nice to see one particular face vanish for ever. 'No, Paul, I won't see you tonight. Let's face it, we're finished.'

'That's just your opinion, Sally. You were fantastic in bed last night.'

'I was stoned out of my mind. You can't say you didn't notice. You took advantage of me.' I did up the last of my buttons. 'And if it's of any interest to you, you were LOUSY!'

I snatched up my dressing-gown, and went my way. My last sight of him was as he stared after me, a look of abject horror on his face. I felt I had at last delivered that knee into his crutch I had promised myself I'd give him.

I returned to the dormitory hut, and had a quick wash. Then I changed from the temporary clothes I had put on into my uniform, and went down to the central complex of buildings. I still had a hangover, but I felt considerably better for getting Paul off my neck.

The day being – as Paul had correctly predicted – the one when many campers were getting ready to leave the next day, I was rushed off my feet. There was the tennis-final to adjudicate, the swimming-relay to help judge (Paul's team didn't win, heh-heh), a beautiful-baby competition to organise, a raffle, a two-hour session of bingo in the theatre and – yes – a knobbly-knees competition to watch.

I was off restaurant-duties that day (Shirley offered to stand in for me all day) and frankly, I don't know how I would have fitted them in.

The evening, fortunately, was quiet. There was a fancy-dress ball in one of the ballrooms, and a farewell concert in the theatre. I was down to work in one of the bars, and it was almost deserted. Every now and then some man would come in from the nearby ballroom and order a massive round, which he carted away on a tray, but generally it was a nice, easy way to pass the most hectic evening of the week.

At about ten o'clock, Alan came in and my heart fluttered. For a few seconds I flattered myself that he had been seeking me out, but he seemed hardly to notice me. He looked very tired.

46

I gave him the double scotch he ordered.

'Bad day in the personnel business?' I said.

He smiled thinly.

'A bad day for everything,' he said. 'What a man like me needs is a drink to help me forget, and girl to help me remember.'

It struck me as a very strange thing to say.

'Do you want to talk about it?' I said. 'I'm not busy at the moment . . . not until the concert finishes.'

Alan looked at me over his glass.

'Not really, thank you.'

Silence fell between us. Just then, a couple of guests drifted in, and I served them. By the time I had finished with them, Alan had drained his glass and was drumming it nervously on the counter.

'Another double,' he said, and gulped it down before I had returned with his change. He pushed the glass forward. 'Same again.'

'You're pushing it a bit heavy, aren't you?' I said.

'And you're being bloody nosey.'

I slammed his money down on the counter, and walked in a huff to the far end of the bar. After all, I reasoned to myself, I was only trying to be sympathetic and understanding in the traditional manner of all good barmaids everywhere. Or was I? After what had happened last night, I was more or less aware of the fact that Alan had made contact with me on a subconscious level. He was more to me now than just a boss. So there was a considerable level of personal affront in my walking away from him. I decided to stay put at the other end of the bar for a bit.

It obviously worked. A few minutes later, Alan sidled along the bar to where I was standing.

'Sally . . . sorry I was rude just then. I'm just not in a very good mood tonight.'

I rewarded him with a big smile.

'That's OK, Alan. Forget it.'

'You're a – '

He was interrupted by two guests who walked over to the bar from the direction of the ballroom. One was dressed as Adam and one was dressed as Eve . . . with body-paint and plastic fig-leaves covering up the appropriate areas. They bought a few whisky macs, loaded them on a tray and carried them back into the ballroom. As the door opened and closed I heard the amplified voice of Jimmy as he was handing out the prizes.

Alan still stood at the bar.

47

'You were going to say?'

'Nothing.' He stared at his glass.

'No . . . go on.'

'OK. I was just going to say that you're a sweet kid, Sally. One of these days we'll learn how to communicate with each other.'

I nodded, smiling at him.

'I think what the trouble is, that we're too like each other. We've got things in common, and people are like magnets: like poles do not attract.' He reached out and squeezed my hand. 'Do you know what I mean?'

'I . . . think so, Alan.' I realised I was beginning to blush. To cover up, I withdrew my hand and turned away, and poured myself a drink. When I turned back again, he was putting down his empty glass.

'I've got to go,' he said. 'I promised I'd go and give Jimmy a hand.'

'And I'm going to be busy in a moment.'

He grinned. 'The camp always comes first. Forget people . . . the camp is the only thing that counts.'

He walked away without another word.

Just then, a large crowd of people poured into the bar, and I guessed that the concert must have finished. Almost simultaneously, several people came in from the ballroom . . . and I found myself being rushed off my feet. I was soon so busy that I forgot about Alan, and had no more time to ponder on his words.

It was a busy few hours – most probably because for a lot of the guests it was the end of their holiday. By consuming vast quantities of alcohol they could console themselves about returning to work on the Monday. I was still washing up glasses at 2 in the morning.

The only black spot was – inevitably – when Paul materialised, full of bright hope and gentle promises. Firmly, and not too politely, I told him to look elsewhere. I was tired . . . and tired of him.

That night, I slept alone and undisturbed. I don't think I would have roused even if Doreen had been entertaining the entire local football team in the next bed.

I never saw Paul again. I didn't know where he lived, I didn't even know his surname. For once a loose end in my life was tied up neatly and finally.

Saturday was another busy day for me. We stewardettes had to abandon most of our usual jobs, and concentrate on the change-over of guests. Standing with a welcoming smile and a friendly manner, we ushered our new holidaymakers through the checking-in process, then saw them to their chalets. But before I started I had to go along, with several of the other girls, for a briefing session in Alan's office.

As we were filing out afterwards, Alan called me back.

'Sally . . . I'm sorry again about last night.'

'It's OK, Alan. I told you. I understand.'

From the expression on his face, I felt certain that he was trying to say something else. I felt I wanted to help him; for I suspected what it was. If my own feelings were any guide, then he was angling round to asking me for a date.

'Yes. Well it's a busy day for all of us.'

'I'd better get out there. I saw a coach driving up.'

'Yes.' Alan looked distinctly nervous. 'Um . . . Sally, I thought one of these days we could have a few drinks together, and I'll try to be a bit more friendly.'

'That'd be nice,' I said, promptly picking up the cue. 'When would you like to make it?'

'Oh . . . one of these days. When we're not so busy.'

He'd had his chance, and let it slip. Perhaps it *was* something else after all. I smiled at him and walked towards the door.

'Are you on the lunch shift today?'

'No, I'm not. I'm on guest-reception all day.'

'Oh, good. Come back to reception in about an hour.'

I went outside. The camp was strangely quiet at the moment. Those people leaving today mostly made an early start, those people arriving hadn't started turning up in droves yet, and those people staying over for a second week were looking after themselves. With no formal programme for the day, apart from a cartoon film-show in the theatre for the kids, most of them went into town to do a bit of shopping, or visited the private beach adjacent to the camp.

After half an hour, the new guests began arriving. A lot came in their own cars, but a large percentage were coming on two special trains from London and the Midlands. When the first of those arrived, we would be really rushed.

The receptionists showed me the drill. After the guests had booked in, I or one of the others was to show the guests how to find their chalet, and call one of the male porters if they needed a hand with their baggage. It all sounded very simple and straightforward. Optimistically, I looked forward to a plain task.

Was I misguided? What I hadn't taken into account was the high percentage of idiots who comprise the human race. Within a very few minutes I was running backwards and forwards like the proverbial blue-arsed fly as I tried to sort out and re-unite separated families, lost kids, apparent duplication of chalets, mislaid luggage, roadways blocked by parked cars, people arriving for the wrong week . . . you name it, I had it.

In the bedlam I quite forgot Alan's request to pop back in and see him after an hour, and it wasn't until five o'clock – when the rush had subsided somewhat – that I remembered. I went into the reception office, slumped down in one of the chairs and put up my poor burning feet. I smoked a cigarette, then feeling renewed walked straight into his office without knocking. Somehow I felt that it was not on business that he wanted to see me.

He looked up in surprise as I marched in, then a grin of relief spread over his face. His desk was almost submerged under a flood of paperwork.

'Hi there . . . still alive?'

'I'm not really sure. You'd better call a doctor and have him check me over.'

'Better than that,' said Alan. 'Tonight you and I ought to take a well-deserved rest. Get completely out of this hell-hole that some people call a holiday centre. What say we go into town and see how the other half lives?'

'That sounds a marvellous idea,' I said. 'But what about the welcoming party? Don't you have to make some kind of appearance there?'

'That's right. And the hell with it, I say.'

'That's a refreshing approach.'

'About bloody time, if you ask me. The season's hardly started, and already I'm browned off with it. Look, let's both knock off now. The other girls can handle any stragglers. I'll pick you up in shanty-town at six.'

I smiled broadly. 'Great.'

I returned to the reception area. With a bit of careful planning, I found a newly-arrived family whose chalet was reasonably near shanty-town, and offered to show them the way. That way I got a lift up the hill in their car. From where they dropped me, it was only a hundred yards extra to walk.

Doreen was lying lazily on her bed when I walked in.

'Where have you been all day?' she said.

'Welcommittee stuff. What about you?'

'Chalet-duty. Changing all the linen. Ouch.'

'What's the matter?'

'My back. How's Alan, then?'

'All right,' I said before I realised. 'You've heard then?'

'It's been all round the camp and back again. You getting on all right with him, then?'

'You sound almost jealous.'

Doreen sat up on her bed.

'Perhaps I am,' she said, and I could see she was more than half-serious. 'I wish I could get a bit of attention from that man ... goodness knows I've flashed it around in front of him enough.'

To emphasise her point she puffed out her chest.

'There,' she said. 'What man in his right mind would turn up his nose at those?'

I looked at Doreen's formidable pair of breasts, jutting through her sweater like a couple of rocket nose-cones. She had a certain point – rather, two certain points – many men would be very turned on by her figure. But not all men would respond to her very positive, almost aggressive, sexual availability. Perhaps Alan just wasn't one of those men who would.

Doreen stood up, and stretched herself in an exaggerated way.

'Sally ... *is* he queer?'

'You mean you aren't certain?'

She looked at me candidly.

'No, I'm not.'

'Well you hang around for a few hours. Alan's taking me out tonight, and I'll be able go give you the answer in the morning. That's if I'm back, of course. Now excuse me, I want to take a shower.'

I walked past her into the bathroom, leaving her standing there with a dumbfounded expression on her face.

CHAPTER 6

ALAN arrived 10 minutes too early for our date. I appreciated that. Even when a man turns up and you're still in the bath, or finishing your make-up, it's nice to feel that he considers you important enough to be early for.

He seemed nervous; much in the way he had appeared in the bar the night before.

When he saw me, he smiled.

51

'Sally, you look absolutely stunning.'

'Thank you very much.' It was nice to get that kind of compliment. I'd found my best dress, although it wasn't much at that. And I suppose that I'd done my best with my make-up, though I'd have appreciated the time to be able to wash my hair.

He led me outside, and I looked around for his car.

'Well, what would you like to do?'

I only wanted one thing: to get out of the camp for a bit, and back into the real world.

'I thought we were going to do the town.'

'That's right . . . what there is of it. Don't expect too much. Priest's Cave is the most exciting thing that happens round here. What's your fancy? Drinks and a dance . . . or a dance and then some drinks? Or would you like a meal? Yes of course, that's what we'll do first.'

'Good. That suits me fine.' I was still looking around for his car. I didn't know he had one, but had just assumed that he had. 'Are we going to drive in to town?'

Alan looked apologetic.

' 'Fraid not. I smashed my car up during the winter, and haven't been able to afford to repair it yet. We'll get a taxi. I've rung for one, and it will be waiting for us.'

So down through the bloodied battlefield of Priest's Cave Holiday Centre we trudged. Several of the new campers were wandering around looking lost, and almost instinctively I felt I ought to offer my assistance. But I was off-duty, and for a bit could forget the job. Let them sort themselves out. They'll find their way round soon enough. I thought of the welcoming party in the ballroom that evening . . . all the funny hats and balloons laid on, the band doing its hokey-cokey thing for the delight of all.

Have a good time, folks, I thought. You're paying for it.

In spite of Alan's outward air of relaxation, I detected that he was terribly tense and nervous. I tended to scorn Doreen's suspicions about him, but it was the one thing I'd heard about him so far that would account for his behaviour. Either that, or he was unbelievably shy. But then, in his job he handled us girls with consummate ease and with very little hard feelings on either side.

As we reached the reception-area, a taxi drew up outside the building.

Alan said: 'Good. That's probably for us.'

We walked over to it, and as we did so the driver reached over and opened the rear passenger door. I climbed in, and Alan followed.

'Hello darlin',' said a familiar voice. 'How's it goin' in Sin City, then?'

'It's Dave, isn't it?'

'Right first time.' He was making no effort to drive off. 'Settling down in the old routine, then?'

'You can forget that for a start,' Alan cut in brusquely. 'She's not one of the girls working the racket.'

Dave shrugged.

'Sorry, Al. I thought they all were. Where can I take you?'

'Er . . . anywhere, Dave. Make it the market square. That's pretty central.'

'Market square it is.' Dave accelerated the engine, and let in the clutch, and we drove smoothly towards the gates of the camp.

Under the noise of the engine, Alan said quietly: 'Dave is in on the racket, as you've probably guessed. If he picks up any likely-looking single men on their way up here, he tips them off, then rings up one of the girls.'

'And he gets a rake-off.'

'A small tip, yes. I don't want to know anything about it. It's bad enough that it happens, and Dave here seems to see me as some kind of super-pimp.'

Dave must have overheard this, for he spoke over his shoulder to us.

'No offence I hope, Al. But it's human nature, isn't it?'

I could sense that Alan was going to respond with some sharp answer, so I reached over and squeezed his hand gently. Instead of replying to Dave, his fingers curled around mine, and he smiled at me. We drove the rest of the way like that . . . our hands resting lightly within each other's. All of a sudden, my whole world seemed to orient around that tiny piece of contact.

As we drove along the sea-front, Alan leaned forward and peered through the side-window.

'There! That'll do, Dave. Drop us here, please.'

Obediently, Dave brought the car to a halt outside a small restaurant, and Alan opened his door. He climbed out first, then helped me out.

'Have it on me, guv,' Dave said, but Alan brushed him aside.

'No . . . I'm paying for this ride, if you don't mind.'

'I don't mind. Just a gesture of goodwill, y'know.'

Alan glanced at the meter, than passed in a few silver coins. Dave acknowledged them cheerfully, and drove away.

'This place do you, Sally?'

'Anywhere at all. Anything to make a change from camp cooking.'

'Ssh!' Alan pressed his finger to his lips.

'What's the matter?'

'Careful what you say. Comparing this high-class establishment with the camp could end you up in a court for defamation. They're very touchy about things like that.'

'Oh . . . sorry.' I wasn't sure whether or not he was joking. I decided to give him the benefit of the doubt, and grinned at him radiantly.

We went inside, and ordered a meal. As he had said, the food was really good. They obviously took great care over their cooking, and the service was polite and unobtrusive.

Afterwards, I felt as if I had eaten well, but not so full that I felt stuffed.

'Fancy that drink now?' Alan said as he settled the bill. I nodded, and he led me across the road towards a pub called *The Prince of Orange*. It didn't look too bad from the outside, but inside it was all plastic and chromium and neon lighting. A jukebox stood threateningly in one corner . . . silent at the moment, but looking as if it would burst into life at the drop of a sixpence. Perhaps Alan caught my unimpressed look, because he shrugged his shoulders apologetically.

'Sorry, Sally, but there isn't really much choice around here. You don't get many pubs with good taste in a small seaside town. This is the sort of place the holidaymakers like . . . so that's what they get.'

'Business must be booming,' I said, glancing round at the nearly empty saloon.

'The bingo halls don't close for another hour. Life on the outside isn't that different from the camp in many respects.'

'You're pretty cynical about the camp, aren't you?' I said, as he bought the drinks, and then I followed him to an empty table. 'Just about every other thing you say is a knock at the place. If you hate it so much, why do you stay there?'

He shrugged.

'Because I can't think of anything else to do, I suppose. During the winter I just bum around in various odd jobs, and I've got used to the camp being my life all summer. I've done nothing else for the last three years.'

'What did you do before that?'

Alan's face clouded over for a second, but it was enough. The

54

way he snapped up the glasses from the table and shot off told me I had hit a sensitive nerve.

I watched him as he stood at the bar, ordering another round. I wasn't sitting in judgement on him, but he was so defensive about himself that it was virtually impossible getting through to him. And yet . . . my feelings for him urged me to persevere. When he came back, it was obvious that he had composed himself but he was determined to steer the conversation on to a safer and less personal topic. He started talking about my work in the camp: did I like it, did I find it tiring, had it turned out to be like I expected?

For his sake I let the conversation ride for several minutes. Then I decided it was time to put a stop to it.

'Alan – we came out to get away from the camp. Remember?'

He grinned. 'Yes, Sally, of course. I'm sorry I started talking shop. I didn't intend to, believe me.'

There was an awkward silence for a while. I decided that this was as good a time as any to start a little probing.

I reached across the table and clasped his hand. He looked up at me, and I could read surprise in his eyes. It was a strange look – surprise, and something which seemed almost grateful, as though he hadn't expected me to make a friendly gesture.

'Do you want to tell me about it?' I said. 'Share a few secrets with a friend and get some of the weight off your chest?'

Alan looked at me in amazement.

'My God, Sally, you're an incredible girl. You seem to be able to read me like a book.'

I smiled. 'As you said yourself last night, it takes one type of person to recognise someone of the same type. I think that you've been badly hurt by someone at some time . . . I can see that because it's happened to me as well.'

'It's a long and boring story,' he said defensively.

I squeezed his hand.

'Never mind that. I'd like to hear it if you'd like to tell me.'

Alan stared at the table-top, lost in thought. I felt that this was the watershed, that from here I had contacted him.

He looked up at me, and I saw that his expression had changed.

'Just now,' he said, 'you asked me what I did before the camp. You wanted to know why I chose to bury myself in a job I hate, in a place I despise.' He took a long swig from his beer. 'I'll tell you.

'You're right, or partially right at least. There was a woman . . . my wife, actually. But it was more than just a broken marriage.

Four years ago I had a different name, and a very different life. I'm not changing the subject, but do you like pop-music, Sally?'

'Yes, I do. Some of it.'

'Then you'll remember Vince Thunder.'

I frowned. The name rang a bell immediately, but I couldn't quite think why. Then, spontaneously, a melody came into my head and I hummed it out loud. 'I know ... "All I Want Is You". Vince Thunder and the Thunderbirds.'

'Right. And 'Good Time Weekend'. And 'Bye Girl Bye'. And a few others. I was Vince Thunder. Six number ones in two and a half years, and two best-selling albums. Enough bookings around the world to keep us going for another five years.'

'If you don't mind me saying so, you don't look much like I remember Vince Thunder.'

Alan laughed.

'I suppose not. I'm three years older, I've lost a bit of weight, I've shaved off my moustache and my hair's a lot shorter. I've changed a lot since then.'

'Why did you give it up? I remember now, there was some mystery. . . .'

'Sally, it was the only life I really loved. It wasn't just the money or the fame . . . I really felt we were in to something. The Thunderbirds were a really good rock band, in spite of what a lot of the critics said. Once we turned down a coast-to-coast tour of the States, simply because we were planning a new album and wanted to sit around letting the thing take shape. It was the music I loved, and that gave me the life. All that and more was taken away from me.'

'But you said there was a woman – your wife. How did she come into it?'

'I don't know if you've ever been in love,' he said, 'but it's like having your whole life and soul bound up in one person who means more to you than money or friends or success . . . or anything else in the world. Well, that was the way I felt about Sandy, my wife. We had just about everything any young couple could have: a beautiful home, a love-affair which seemed to be straight out of the story-books and more money than we knew what to do with. I met Sandy when I was struggling along with a group playing in pubs. She stuck with me faithfully then, and she stuck with me when I started to hit the big-time.'

'So what happened?' I said.

'You know how the groupies hang around bands? You know the stories about orgiastic parties after every gig? Well . . . to a

56

certain extent, everything you've heard is true, but only to that extent. There are more married men playing in bands these days, and after a while the groupies get the message and only go after the single ones. I rarely came into contact with the groupies, and didn't regret it, either.

'Then, to cut a long story short, one of the groupies working the circuit got herself pregnant. She saw me as a soft touch . . . the Thunderbirds were at the height of their success at the time . . . and laid a paternity suit on me. Even though there was no truth or substance in her claim, Sandy stopped trusting me, and from that moment we started to break apart.

'The big crunch came on the day of the court-case. I was contesting the suit, of course, and wanted Sandy to come and hear the facts. But she wouldn't. During the case, the girl was closely cross-examined, and I had a certain amount of evidence on my side . . . like a blood-test, for example. In the end, the girl broke down in tears and admitted that I had never been anywhere near her.

'You've no idea how happy I was when I left that courtroom. I rushed straight home to tell Sandy the news . . . and there she was in bed with one of the group's roadies. It was her way of getting revenge, you see – evening up the score as it were. But she couldn't wait until after the case . . . didn't wait to see if I was really guilty.'

'Couldn't you have forgiven her?' I said.

Alan shook his head sadly.

'No . . . because I was stupid and I let my male ego overcome the love I had for my wife. I just couldn't forgive her, and by the time I could it was too late. I went off with the band, and we played some really hard gigs. I drowned myself in the music . . . and in the end I pushed the rest of the group too far. I was hitting speed by then, and making time with the groupies. This went on for about six months. Then I zonked out completely, and came round in a hospital bed. I transferred to a private clinic and they kept me there for nearly a year. When they finally let me out, Vince Thunder was good and dead . . . and my wife was gone. The divorce was finalised last year.'

Alan drained the rest of his beer, and lit a cigarette.

'So that's about it, in a nutshell,' he said. 'The job at the camp was offered to me through some friends in the entertainment business, and it seemed like a good place to hide from the world. Just like I said before: people go to holiday camps because they are trying to escape from reality.'

I stared at Alan, and he stared back. I was seeing him in a totally new light; and I wished he had only told me this earlier. Suddenly he became complete, rounded-out. He was a human being . . . not just some cipher with a name and a job, and a mysterious past that was left to everyone else to speculate about.

Noises intruded, and the juke-box started up. I looked round the pub, saw that it was filling up with people. A group of young men wearing cowboy hats stood at the bar, shouting for service.

I said: 'Come on, Alan. Let's get out of this place.'

He stood up.

'Let's go and have that dance. I feel like it now.'

'Do you know anywhere?'

He grinned.

'I can't vouch for it, as I've never been myself, but one or two of the girls have told me about a discotheque that's supposed to be here somewhere.'

'We shouldn't have much difficulty finding it in a place this size.'

'Right. It's worth a try.'

He took my hand, and led me out into the street. The night was clear, windless and very warm. I clung to his arm as we walked from the front towards the centre of town.

CHAPTER 7

WE were directed to the club by a policeman, and found it in a part of town well away from that habituated by the holiday-makers. It was in a cellar below some shops in a sidestreet.

As we went in the door, we felt waves of heat rising up, and could feel the floor shaking in time to the bass rhythms of the drums and guitar.

On a stage at the far side was a group going full-pelt in the middle of a fast rock number. As soon as we were on the floor, Alan started dancing, and I joined in.

After five minutes, the group showed no signs of slowing up and I was just beginning to enjoy myself.

Alan put his hands on my shoulders and pulled my face towards his.

'What do you think of the group?' he bellowed down my ear.

'I think they're very good,' I replied in like fashion.

'I think they're *bloody* good,' Alan shouted.

We carried on dancing until the number came to its climax, and the group stopped playing. To the disappointment of both of us, they put down their instruments and walked off stage.

'We came too late,' Alan said. 'I could have taken hours of that kind of playing.'

'You think they're good then?'

'I told you. They're bloody good.'

'As good as the Thunderbirds?'

Alan grinned. 'Not quite. But bloody near.'

Just then, the club's disc-jockey put on a track from an album, and more music flooded in.

A young man stood by himself nearby, and Alan turned to him.

'Excuse me,' he shouted over the noise. 'That group . . . who are they?'

The young man said something in reply, but neither of us could hear.

'What?' Alan said.

'They're called Maxima Culpa . . . they're a local group.'

'Thanks.' Alan turned to me. 'Fancy a drink?'

I nodded, but the young man caught Alan's arm.

'Maxima Culpa,' he shouted. 'What do you think?'

'I like them. Are they going to play any more?'

'After the break.'

'Good.'

This exchange of information out of the way, we parted company with the young man and went to the bar. After a couple more drinks we went back into the main area. I detected that a subtle change had come over Alan. He led me over to the stage, and sat on the floor in front of it. I gathered that he wasn't intending to do any more dancing, but that we were going to do some listening. In about five minutes, a couple of the members of the group came on to the stage, and began to fiddle with their instruments and amplifiers.

Suddenly, Alan stood up.

'Come with me, Sally.'

He climbed up on to the small stage, and went over to the guitarist.

'Hey, man . . . d'you mind if I sit in with you for a couple of numbers?'

The guitarist looked at him in surprise.

'No, I don't mind. What do you play?'

'Guitar.'

'What kind? Bass? Rhythm?'

'Any kind. I could come in as additional rhythm guitar, if you like.'

'You done group-work?'

'Yes.'

'Got an axe?'

Alan looked slightly worried. 'No . . . I haven't.'

'That's OK. We've got a spare. I'll get one of the roadies to dig it out for you.'

'You sure you don't mind?'

'No we don't mind, man. What's your name?'

I squeezed Alan's hand, and went back and sat on the floor. He was lost to me. As the other members of the group came on stage, Alan was introduced to them.

Somebody came in, and gave him a guitar, and he tuned it up and plugged in to one of the amplifiers. I was watching him . . . not watching Alan Spiers, personnel administrator at the camp, but watching a young man trying to find himself again.

Maxima Culpa started their first number, with Alan sitting at the side of the stage. He didn't join in this one.

That number finished, and they played three more. All this time, Alan sat by himself, listening acutely to the music.

Then the lead-guitarist came to the microphone.

'Er . . . we got us a new member tonight. Don't shout him off the stage at once, 'cos he's a bit nervous.' The guitarist grinned nervously himself, looking round at the rest of the group. 'We're gonna do an old number now, a Chuck Berry song. *Johnny B. Goode*.'

Someone stamped his foot four times . . . and the number started. I realised Alan was on his feet, and playing. And my God, how he was playing! Maxima Culpa had sounded good before . . . now they sounded magnificent. Underlying their hoarse, repetitive riffs there was now a fulness and harshness that thrilled the very soul. I watched Alan as he played. He was standing well to the back of the stage, out of the limelight, but his head was bent over the borrowed guitar in total absorption with his music.

The singer went through the verse, and into the chorus. There was a long guitar-break from the lead, and then more verse. Then the lead-guitar stopped playing, and the rhythm section played on by itself. There were now two rhythm-guitars – Alan on one – bass, and drums. Alan stepped forward hesitantly, never letting up on the driving pace of his playing. The sound came out and surrounded us, threatening to rupture our eardrums. I found I was standing up, waving my arms. Behind me, people had stopped dancing and were crowding forward to the stage.

The lead-guitar came in again, and brought the number to a deafening climax.

Around me, the club exploded into applause.

The guitarist came forward to the microphone.

'Thank you everybody. We gotta play a few old numbers, 'cos our new guitarist doesn't know our own numbers. Give him some appreciation . . . Alan Spiers!'

Alan nodded to the crowd, who gave him a healthy burst of applause to himself.

There was a movement at my side, and I found a young man in dark glasses beside me.

'You with that guy?'

'Yes.'

'Who is he? His face is familiar.'

'He's Alan Spiers.'

He shook his head.

'Doesn't mean anything to me. But he plays like an old-timer.'

'Why are you interested?'

'I'm from the management agency who handle Maxima. I've been around a long time. You sure that's his real name? He hasn't played under another name?'

I said: 'He used to play as Vin – '

My words were lost in a renewed barrage of music from the group. I was glad, because I had regretted my words almost as soon as I started them. Alan had confided that secret to me . . . and it wasn't mine to divulge.

The second number was an old Beatles song: *I Saw Her Standing There*. Once again, Alan took a back place in the group, not trying to steal anything from the others. But it was clear that it was in him the crowd was interested. I knew it wasn't only my own interest in him making me think this. The crowd was listening to the music, whereas before they had only danced. Maxima Culpa had been transformed from a good, exciting group into one which took the audience by the throat and screamed exhilaration into its face.

After that number, Alan took off his guitar, nodded to the

others and tried to leave the stage.

But the audience wouldn't let him. They cried *More!* until they were hoarse, stamping their feet in a steady beat until Alan walked back on again. This time, even the other members of the group applauded him.

The young man at my side said: 'You were going to tell me who he'd played with.'

I shook my head. 'You wouldn't know the group. Just a small semi-pro band that never made it.'

'I don't believe it. With a player like that, any group would make it.'

I was saved from further conversation by the music starting up again, this time with Alan standing well to the front of the stage. I had difficulty recognising the number at first, then placed it as an old Status Quo track: *Mean, Mean Girl.* After the first few bars Alan stepped forward to the microphone, and began singing the words. It was a deep, raucous voice, totally unlike his speaking voice. Again, I found myself thrilling towards him, so excited that perspiration was soaking my clothes.

The guitar-solo came, and this time it was Alan. His fingers flashed across the fingerboard, seeming to play six notes for every one that was struck.

As the song ended, the audience surged forward, screaming for more and more . . . .

I glanced at the young man beside me.

'I thought I got a good group playing for me,' he said. 'But with that guy I got myself the greatest in England.'

I was so excited I could hardly answer, and instead just grinned broadly.

'I'm gonna sign him if it's the last thing I do.'

I made to answer, but he moved away towards the side of the stage. I was looking at Alan again, watching as he spoke to the lead guitarist. A moment later, the next number started.

And then another. And half a dozen more.

The last number was an extended version of Larry Williams' *Slow Down*, for which the group did almost anything except slow down. By the time they came crashing to a finish I thought I was going to die from excitement. Alan was soaked in perspiration, his hair matted to his face. His shirt clung wetly to his body, and his whole expression was one of total exhilaration.

The audience began chanting for more, and their feet stamped in unison . . . but the set was finished. The management switched on the house-lights, and the guitarist raised his hand in farewell.

Alan lifted off the guitar, and laid it by the amplifier.

I pushed through the crowd, and made my way to the side. Alan stepped down from the stage, and grinned at me.

I couldn't say anything. All I could do was hug him to me.

'Say, man, could I have a word with you?'

I turned. It was the man with dark glasses.

'Sure . . . wait here a moment will you, Sally?'

Alan went with the rest of the group towards a door, and disappeared through it. I sat down on the edge of the stage, waiting while the club emptied. I was the only one there when Alan came back to me a few minutes later.

'Hi. Sorry about that, Sally.'

'You finished?'

'Yeah . . . come on, let's go.'

We walked through the club, up the stairs and into the street. Suddenly, everything seemed unreal. My ears were singing with the noise they had just suffered, and my whole body was tingling with the after-effects of the music.

It had been hot inside the club, and I expected to feel the cold as soon as we got into the air. But the night was still muggy and warm, and although I shivered for a moment I soon felt warm. We walked towards the front, soon coming out on the promenade. It was strangely deserted. No traffic went past, no holidaymakers walked by. I looked at my watch, and saw to my utter surprise that it was after half-past one.

'What did that man want?'

'Oh . . . him. He's the group's manager. Wanted me to join the band.'

'Are you going to?'

'No . . . I'd like to, but I've finished with music.'

'But Alan! You're fantastically good. You should never have left.'

'I don't know. I'm a bit old for that sort of thing now.'

'How old are you, grandpa?'

'Twenty-five.'

'A has-been before you're thirty.' I was trying to mock him.

' 'Fraid so,' Alan said.

'What do you think of the group?'

'Maxima Culpa? They're really good. I can't understand how they haven't made it. Joe, the manager, was telling me that they play a lot of gigs, but that they're all in this area. They can't break out into the main scene. They should, they're good enough.'

I stopped walking, and turned to face him.

'Alan . . . you know what I'm thinking. Throw in your job at the camp. You're wasted there. Join the band, and get back to music.'

Alan just shook his head slowly.

'No, Sally. I've been bitten once. I'd dearly love to . . . but I'm afraid to.'

'Did you tell them?'

'About Vince Thunder?'

'Yes.'

'Yes . . . they know.'

'What happened?'

'Joe doubled the price he offered me.'

I said: 'But aren't you tempted?'

Alan gripped my hand very gently, but firmly.

'I'm tempted, Sally.'

He led me down some wooden steps to the beach. The tide was a long way out, and we could hear the noise of the water as a gentle murmuring in the background. In a few minutes we were away from the town and walking in almost complete darkness before some cliffs. Beneath our feet, the sand was dry and warm. I looked up. The sky was clear, and a half moon shone down. I wondered how long this hot weather would last; trusted in an instinctive way that it would last for ever.

By my side walked a strange man. Gone was the gloomy, faintly pessimistic and cynical Alan; here instead was a younger man, a surer man. Gone was the virtual adolescence of his courtship of me; instead was a purpose and a confidence that only inspired me. I knew where we were walking . . . and I knew why.

We came at last to a narrow cove, which lay between two high cliffs. We walked into it, and lay down on the sand still warm from the day's sun. Alan was close beside me . . . and then he was kissing me.

At first his lips were soft on mine, though sensuous. As he felt me respond, his mouth grew more demanding, more insistent. I turned my body so that his hand moved . . . felt his fingers touch my breast. He touched me with a sense of gentle wonderment; without passion.

For a long time our lovemaking was like that. We were demanding nothing of each other. We loved each other, and caressed each other in a way that said everything was all right, nothing else could affect us.

I sat up to allow him to unzip my dress, and felt that sensation of restraining cloth falling loose on my body. I pulled my arms from the sleeves, then lay back again as he slid the dress down my legs. Alan's hands crept round to my back, fumbling with the clasp of the bra. As it came free, my breasts swelled out to him and I felt a thrill of desire. I was free. I was wanted. I was happy.

Alan's hands cupped my breasts, squeezing then gently. He kneaded the soft flesh, corrugating it with his fingers. Bending down to me, he took one of my nipples in his mouth and kissed it until it hardened into a small lump in which all my pent-up desires were centred. His tongue darted like that of a snake, across my stomach, down to where my tights cut into the soft flesh of my belly.

Gradually, carefully, he pulled at the material, slipping it with my panties down my legs and off my feet.

I lay nude on the sand. I found my legs were writhing, rubbing sensuously across the loose sand. I wanted to bury myself, take Alan with me. He moved away from me for a moment, and I could see his dark figure silhouetted against the sky as he took off his clothes. His skin glowed white. I wanted to kiss him all over, feel and taste every inch of his flesh.

'Listen to the waves,' he said quietly, as he lay alongside me once more. They seemed nearer now, and the gentle sussuration must have been reaching me unconsciously, for I found the sound to be entirely erotic. 'We'll make love slowly, in time with the sea.'

He lowered his face to my body, and I felt his breath in my hair . . . cooling the warmth that swelled there. I reached out for him, found his male strength and enclosed it in my palm. I was becoming giddy, whirling as if drunken.

Now the sea took on a new note . . . it was more rhythmic, more driving. I realised that my ears were tricking me, feeding me a false echo of the music in that club. For Alan's strength I saw the long fingerboard of a guitar, his hand moving up and down in an unmistakable way. So too were the waves, and now so was Alan's hand on my body.

I raised my knees, held them wide. As Alan rolled over me, he was encompassed within me, as man is taken into woman. My body was straining, reaching out like the puckered lips of a mouth about to kiss. I thrust myself towards him as I wished him to thrust himself into me. I engulfed him in my passion as my body engulfed his driving force. It came into me, filling me, bursting its power into my very being.

I listened to the sea, and the surf crashed within me, foaming, bursting, and then receding.

We dressed. We walked. We found a taxi. And then we were back in the camp.

We had been gone only a few hours. Just as both Alan and I had escaped in the first place to the camp, so too we had escaped from it for a few hours. But now we were back, surrounded by its tinsel and bright lights, the forced happiness of the campers.

It looked different somehow, and yet still the same.

I was depressed by the camp, saw it now as a place with unpleasant associations.

Alan held me in his arms outside the shanty town dormitory.

'Sally . . . I would love nothing more than to have you sleep with me tonight.'

'Then why can't we do it?'

He looked round helplessly. 'How would you prefer it: me with you in there, or you with me in my hut?'

I knew what he meant. We could never be private.

'OK. I'll see you in the morning.'

Alan kissed me, and then looked at me intently.

'I hope so, Sally. I really hope so. But then I think I fear you.'

With that he turned away, and walked off into the dark. In that brief instant he had reverted to his former type: abrupt, enigmatic. I could not see those words being uttered by the man I saw with his guitar, the man who had made love to me only a few minutes before on that beach.

Puzzled – and disturbed – I crept into the dormitory, slipped off my clothes and fell into bed. All was quiet. I lay for a long time awake, trying to sort out the vivid impressions I still carried from those memorable few hours in the town.

Then sleep came, and it was a deep sleep unbroken by dreams.

I awoke with the other girls, pretending to join in the morning bedlam of fighting for mirror-space, of hastily tidying up the hut.

Doreen came over to me, as I sat on my bed brushing my hair.

'Well?'

'Well what?'

'Who . . . Alan?'

'Of course. Who d'you think I mean, Genghis Khan?'

'He was all right.'

'Is that all? What did you do?'

I smiled at her enigmatically, in a way I knew would mystify and infuriate her.

'We went into town.'

'And . . .?'

'We had a meal. Then we had a drink. Then we went dancing. Then we went for a walk. Then we came home. Then I got into bed. On my own.'

'Ha!' She contrived to sound as if I had proved something, but I wasn't to be drawn on the subject. I cherished the memory of the night before, and I wasn't going to spoil it by talking about it.

I walked down to the restaurant with her, keeping half an eye open for a sight of Alan. But he seemed to be lying low, because one of his assistants briefed us on our work for the day.

I worked my way without any untoward disaster through the breakfast shift, then went by myself to the staff canteen. I was sitting there, enjoying my second cup of coffee while I pored over the *Daily Mirror* when Doreen came in. Something about her expression stopped me in mid-thought, and I stared at her.

'Doreen . . . whatever's the matter?'

'I thought you'd know if anyone did. Don't you know what's happened?'

'No I don't. What's going on?' I knew. It was Alan.

'You know. It's Alan.'

I shook my head, blankly, willing away the news she was about to break me.

'Is he . . . all right?'

Doreen shrugged, and held my arm as I stood up.

'No one knows. He disappeared in the middle of the night, after wrecking his office. Nobody knows where he'd gone, and there's been a. . . .'

I didn't hear the rest of her words.

A confusion of impressions flooded through my mind . . . but they were of two main kinds. One of utter distress that Alan had left; the other a heady exhilaration because I knew where he had gone. And why.

Though I would have no idea how to find him.

Doreen caught me as I fainted.

I became aware of fingers snapping in front of my face, then an acrid smell of ammonia.

I coughed, and looked round. I found myself on that bright-blue water-bed, with Trevor looking at me anxiously.

'What . . . happened?' I said.

'You passed out. You were going along nicely, and then your eyes closed and you passed out.'

'But why?'

'I think I know the reason. It's a fairly common psychological phenomenon. You were identifying closely with your narrative, and when your memory came of fainting, you followed suit.'

'My memory?' I looked at him in some alarm. 'But it's not a memory. This is more real than that.'

'Yes, yes. But for our purposes the description as a memory will do. This is what you are here for, are you not? To recover your memory.'

'But . . . I'm not *remembering* this. It is how it happened.'

Trevor stood up, and put aside the bottle of smelling-salts.

'Nevertheless, it is your only recall. Now then, what happened to Alan? I must say I am very curious.'

'What happened . . .? To *who* . . .?'

'Alan. Alan Spiers. The – er – young man you encountered during your stay at the camp.'

'Camp?' I said. 'What camp?'

'The holiday-camp.'

'Oh . . . that.'

It was a weird sensation and one I find hard to talk about even now. At one moment I had been re-living the experiences at the camp, and the next I was back in Trevor's office. And yet, during the time I had been telling him about the camp, it had felt so real to me that I was almost carrying out the actions I described.

'Are you feeling better?'

'Yes thanks. What happened? Am I ill?'

Trevor laughed, and stood up. He opened a packet of cigarettes and offered me one.

'No . . . you're not ill, Sally. Not physically ill, that is. But you are in a condition we analysts refer to as a fugue. That is, you are reverting to former experiences and re-living them. This is very natural, and very encouraging. I think you are well on the way to recovery of your memory.'

A sudden, rather alarming thought came to mind.

'Er . . . these experiences. Am I reliving them *all*?'

Trevor looked at me shrewdly.

'Yes, Sally. All of them.' He walked over to his desk, and opened the lid of a taperecorder. He pressed a button, and the spools whizzed round. He pressed another button and –

– *kneaded the soft flesh, corrugating it with his fingers. Bending down to me, he took one of my nipples in his mouth and* –

'Turn it off!' I said, blushing furiously.

He complied, and closed the lid.

'I'm sorry if that embarrasses you, but I feel you must know the true extent of your memory-recall. You must be encouraged by this. Your progress is far faster than I had dared hope. As for the nature of your memories . . . well, you must appreciate that I am a doctor, and that in my work I must necessarily learn a great deal of detail about my patients. I assure you, I listen to your revelations in a purely professional sense. Naturally, nothing you have said will be repeated outside this room, and I will go so far as to say that when your treatment is complete I shall be happy to let you take the tapes away yourself to have them destroyed.'

I drew on my cigarette.

'Thank you . . . doctor.'

He shook his head. 'Please . . . call me Trevor, as you have always done.'

I nodded silently.

It was taking a bit of getting used to, finding out that all my inner thoughts and desires were pouring out of me, and into his ears and recorder.

He stubbed out his cigarette, and stood up.

'I think Sally that we must call it a night at this point. You have stayed far too late, constructive though this has been. You must allow me to get my secretary to drive you home.'

'That's all right,' I said. 'I can go on the Tube.'

'No . . . I insist. Do you know the time?'

I looked at my watch. It was nearly eleven o'clock. I must have been out for hours.

He was pressing a button on his intercom.

'Damn . . . she must have left. I'll take you home myself.'

'No, really. . . .'

'I insist.'

And that was the end of the argument. A few minutes later, he took me downstairs to the garage, sat me firmly in the front seat of his Daimler, and drove me home to a very curious Mum and Dad.

I went straight to bed, and slept well.

In the morning, I sat with Mum having a cup of coffee after breakfast.

'Mum . . .' I said slowly. 'Do you remember that time you took me to a holiday-camp in Devon?'

She looked at me curiously.

'Holiday-camp, dear? I don't remember that.'

'You know. We went when I was very small. I must have been about six or seven.'

'No, love, I think you must be imagining it. Don't you remember, we always went to your Aunt Elsie's in Sidmouth when you were little.'

'Yes . . . that's right.' I shrugged. It was very odd.

The following week, I went back to Trevor's for the next session. Just as a precaution I warned Mum I might be late, and that I'd ring her before I left.

During the week, I'd done my damndest to remember more about my memories of the camp, but annoyingly I'd been unable to think of a thing. It was convenient to attribute everything to my amnesia, but I knew deep inside me that that wasn't the answer.

I knew – I *knew* – that the experiences I was describing were not part of that 18-month gap in my life, but where they came from I hadn't the faintest idea. But they were so real to me, so concrete and vivid that I knew they couldn't be invented. It was all very puzzling.

Trevor greeted me cordially, and took me straight in to his consulting room. The water-bed was ready, and I lay back on it hoping the train of memories would start at once. Frustratingly, they stayed elusive. After half an hour of straining after them, Trevor advised me to relax. I got off the water-bed, and sat beside him on a chaise-longue in front of the bookcase.

'Would you like one of those pills?' he said. 'They won't work any magic, but they may help.'

'They helped before.'

'Yes . . . but I was hoping we wouldn't have to resort to them.

It could happen that you would come to rely on them to spur your memory, and in time we might be able to extract nothing from you at all.'

'OK, I'll try again,' I finished my coffee, and went back to the water-bed.

'Just relax, Sally. Think of nothing at all . . . and close your eyes.'

I did as he said, and listened to him moving about quietly behind me. There was a click, a soft humming noise, and then Trevor was beside me.

'Listen to this. It may help.'

I didn't open my eyes, but listened as he directed. There was another clicking noise, and then I hear the soft sound of a girl's voice – my voice – coming from the speaker of the recorder.

I heard my description of Alan playing in the discotheque, then the love-making on the beach, then the return to the camp. Images jumped into my mind. Then I heard Doreen's words, telling me that Alan had wrecked his office and left the camp.

The vision had returned. . . .

CHAPTER 8

IT was the shock of Alan's sudden departure which had laid me out. When I came round, I was asking myself again and again: *But why . . .?* It was not that I couldn't understand him – I knew perfectly well why he would prefer a return to the life of a pop-singer to working in the camp – but why had he not said anything to *me*? It was that that hurt so much.

Doreen sat with me there in the staff canteen, her hand resting consolingly on mine. In a few minutes I had recovered myself.

Suddenly, I felt comforted. Perhaps Alan suspected we understood each other too well. He knew that only I, of all the people in the camp, would guess what had happened. In a sense, his very act of abrupt departure was a secret message to me.

'*You know where I've gone, Sally. I'll be in touch. See you? . . .*'

I sat up straight, and pulled my hand away from Doreen's. She looked at me in some surprise.

'Got a cigarette?' I said.

'Are you all right, Sally?'

'Yes . . . of course. Why shouldn't I be? Let's have some more coffee.'

'But. . . . Just now, you passed out when I told you about Alan. I thought you were dead from shock!'

'Oh . . . that,' I said airily. 'It was nothing to do with him. He kept me out a bit late last night, and I'm tired. It's warm in here, that's all.'

She looked at me with a puzzled frown, then fished in her handbag and passed me a cigarette.

'I'm sorry, Sally. I honestly thought you were upset about Alan.'

'But why? We just had a date last night. That's all. There's nothing special between us. In fact,' I leaned forward confidentially, 'I suspected he might do something like that.'

Doreen's interest was obviously aroused.

'What did he say? Did he tell you he was going to wreck his office?'

I nodded. 'And I know where he is.'

'Come on, Sally, tell me.'

'Keep it a secret?' I knew in half an hour it'd be all round the camp.

She nodded fiercely.

'OK, but you mustn't let this get out. He got the sack yesterday, and still had a week's notice to serve. That's why he took me out. He said he'd had enough of the camp, and wanted to get away for a bit.'

'But why was he sacked?' Doreen was leaning towards me, right across the table.

'Do you remember that girl who was staying at the camp last week? A rather tall, attractive blonde? She was with her husband.'

Doreen frowned. 'Can't say I do. . . .'

'You must have seen her. She had the most fantastic figure. In Chalet K. 147? Anyway . . . it was her.'

'What was her?'

'She was the one he was caught with.'

'Gosh! What were they doing?'

'Can't you imagine? Apparently, one of the security-guards saw them swimming in the nude in the pool in the early hours of Friday morning. He reported it to one of the directors, who went down to the pool in person. By the time he got there, they were . . . you know. . . .'

I thought Doreen's eyes were going to fall from their sockets.

'Gosh!' she said again.

'So you were wrong, it seems,' I said. 'He wasn't bent at all.'

'No . . . he couldn't have been. I wish I'd. . . .'

'You wish you'd what?'

'Nothing.' Doreen stood up quickly, and looked elaborately at her watch. 'I must dash, Sally. Got to be on the sports-field in five minutes.'

'OK. I'll see you later. And don't forget . . . keep mum, won't you?'

'You can trust me. I won't tell a soul.'

I grinned at her. 'See you later, Doreen.'

'See you.'

She practically galloped from the canteen, and I sat back in my chair smiling to myself.

The pain of Alan's absence had not yet grown in me. I still could hardly believe that he had left. But even so, I felt warm inside. I was almost glad that he had not said anything to me. His very silence was a kind of pact. I wanted desperately to see him again, but I knew it would not be long. He would contact me, I knew that. . . .

By lunchtime, three separate people had come up to me and confided that they 'knew' why Alan had left so hurriedly. Each time, the story I heard grew slightly more sensational.

By teatime, it was common knowledge that Alan had been found with at least six naked girl guests in the swimming-pool.

At the very least, the suspicion that he was homosexual was well and truly scotched.

But of course, somebody was bound sooner or later to do some checking, and when the story was expressly denied by a member of the management then my harmless deception was at an end.

Doreen collared me when I was serving behind the bar in the ballroom.

'You've heard what they've said?' she asked suspiciously.

I looked distressed.

'I only told you what Alan told me. Perhaps he has some other reason for wanting to leave.'

She shrugged.

'Oh well, there are plenty more personnel managers in the world. Perhaps the new one will be more interested in me.'

'There's a new one coming?'

'Of course. I hear he'll be starting later in the week. Wonder what he's like?'

And that was the way in which Doreen's interest in Alan died.

73

As suddenly and completely as that. Obviously, she had secretly coveted him for a long time . . . but she saw him only as a potential lay. Not a person. Now he had gone, and there was someone coming to take his place, her interest had been transferred.

In the next couple of days, few people mentioned Alan again. By the end of the week, I felt I was probably the only person in the camp who remembered him. Except the management, of course, who'd had to have the office cleaned up, the typewriter repaired, the leg on the table replaced. . . .

Sure enough, the new personnel man arrived on the Thursday following Alan's sudden departure. He was a much older man than Alan had been, and one much more difficult to get on with. He insisted from the start on being addressed as 'Mr Harris' and laid down several new stringent rules about behaviour.

Everyone on the staff was concerned about this, though there was a strong feeling that when he settled in things would be easier. As far as the holidaymakers were concerned, nothing would have appeared to change. Life went on in the camp as normal, but behind the scenes things were far from what they had been.

Mr Harris seemed intent on instigating a reign of terror. In the first week, two of the girls were sacked. *We* all knew why they'd been caught 'entertaining' male guests, but it was announced that their discipline and service was below standard.

Of course, everyone became much more careful. Those girls working the racket went to great pains to be not seen talking to the men during working hours, and took to making up all sorts of complicated cover-stories and excuses. What Alan had told me was turning out to be true. No one could actually stop liaisons between the male customers and the girls, all they could do was drive it further underground. But if that was the way the management wanted it – preserving their jealously guarded image as a 'nice', family holiday-camp – that was the way they got it.

Suddenly, instead of being discreet allies, the security guards became tacit enemies, and feelings ran high. No longer was it possible to bribe them to look the other way – indeed, one girl was actually sacked for trying to slip a guard a fiver – and now they became a kind of secret police, working with renewed vigour to make up for the fact that their little bit of tax-free income had been taken away from them.

It didn't make sense to me, because the whole atmosphere at the camp was geared to a feeling of bonhomie and all's right with the world. Now things weren't right any more, and the standards

74

discipline and service *did* start to drop off.

For my own part, I was involved only slightly. I came under ¢e almost universal suspicions of the ever-vigilant security-¿ards, and many of the girls – particularly Doreen – took out ¢eir feelings of hard-done-by on me, by bemoaning their re-¡ricted freedoms at great and boring length.

I had a clear conscience about this, because I'd never been ¿volved, even before Mr Harris arrived. That doesn't mean to ¿y I was pious about it...the girls had long since abandoned hope ¿r me...but simply that as far as I was concerned, Mr Harris's ¿ign of terror restricted my freedom not at all.

If it weren't for the fact that I was eating my heart out for Alan, ¿doubt if I'd have even noticed the presence of someone else in ¿s place.

And eating my heart out I really was.

The weeks slipped by, and there was no word from him.

At first I used to hurry down to the office in the mornings to ¿e if there was any post for me...and when the phone rang in ¿e dormitory hut I was always the one who rushed over to pick ¿ up. But after the first two weeks after Alan left, I no longer did ¿ese things.

He did not get in touch with me. He did not write. He did not ¿hone. Slowly, the realisation was growing in me that by leaving ¿ithout saying anything he *had* been running away. From me....

When I first realised that it wasn't going to be he who would ¿et in touch, I did what I could to find him. I suspected he was ¿ith that group, Maxima Culpa, and went one drizzly afternoon ¿ the club in town. No, they said, Maxima Culpa no longer ¿layed there. They'd been re-organised, changed their manager, ¿oved to London. No, they didn't know where I could contact ¿em.

I got talking one evening to Don, the pianist in the camp-band, ¿e lent me a musical trade-paper, and I scoured it, hoping to ¿nd a mention of Maxima Culpa...but no luck.

It was about then that I realised that Alan was hiding from me, ¿nd the feeling of blank despair took over.

All this time I was going through the motions at the camp. I ¿rganised spot-prizes at the dances, took the kids for country ¿alks, served breakfasts, lunches, dinners, acted as caller in the ¿amp bingo-hall, helped out behind the bars, ran the knobbly-¿nees contest...and all the while kept up my bright, brittle ¿mile for the benefit of the holidaymakers.

But inside, my feelings were a universe away. The world was

a bleak place, rendered grey by Alan's absence. For a few day
the weather turned bad, and as the holidaymakers sloshed fron
one muddy part of the camp to another, I thought I'd throw i
the whole thing altogether. Then the weather turned sunn
again . . . but my feelings remained the same.

I stayed at the camp, because it was my only link with Alan
If I moved from the camp, then he would never be able to fine
me.

So I hung on, the prospect of seeing him again growing eve
slimmer.

There was no longer any doubt in my mind: I loved Alan witl
every cell in my body. I wanted him with me, yearned for jus
one fleeting glimpse of him.

I realised I was drinking too much, but didn't care.

Whenever I worked behind one of the bars I was confronted
with the temptation to take every drink offered. What I had don
in the past – like most of the other girls – was to smile nicely a
the customer, say 'thank-you' and add a few pence on to hi
round, pocketing the money later. Now, however, I took th
drink when it was offered to me, and drank it quickly to be ready
for the next one.

On a typical evening behind one of the bars in the ballroom, .
could expect to have bought for me at least half a dozen spirits . .
and often more. As a result, I was usually pickled when the shif
finished.

That suited me fine: I didn't have to think about anything
and it helped me sleep.

Doreen said to me once: 'You're drinking too much, Sally.

'I know. Fun, isn't it?'

'Yeah . . . great. What's the matter love? Want to tell me abou
it?'

I shook my head. 'No, Doreen. It's nothing. I've just acquired
a taste for it, that's all. I'm not hitting the bottle or anything.'

'It's not . . . ?'

'Not what?'

Doreen frowned. 'Well, it isn't anything to do with Alan
Spiers, is it?'

'No, it's not,' I said firmly. 'I told you, he was just a one-nigh
date. I've almost forgotten him. Hey . . . who was that fantasti
looking guy you were with last night?'

The subject deftly changed, Doreen threw off her guise a
mother-comforter and brightened considerably. She launched

into a long description of her previous night's mark, and my troubles were quickly forgotten. By her at least.

Of course, she had hit the nail right on the head. Alan Spiers it was, and Alan Spiers it remained.

About a month after his disappearance, I was well into my nightly habit of having one or two over the eight, and Alan was, indeed, quite forgotten for much of the time.

Then one particular Thursday night came along.

Thursdays were always rather odd evenings at the camp. In the early evening there was a cartoon-show for the children, and then afterwards the ballroom was given over to old-time dancing, and in the discotheque a guest group from outside came in. (It was too much to dare to hope that a certain group by the name of Maxima Culpa would play there . . . and it was so. I scoured the booking-forms one day in the camp office, but they were not down to play, and so I forgot about this idea). Thursdays were therefore split into two: those who liked Military Two-Steps and St. Bernard Waltzes stayed in the ballroom, and those who like frugging to the latest funky boogie band from London headed for the discotheque. But for a lot of people, the camp didn't hold much of interest. Some went into town for the evening, but a lot of people headed for the bars.

On this particular Thursday evening, five weeks after Alan's departure, I was working in one of the bars. I was offered a lot of drinks, consumed them all . . . and by the time the steel shutter was rattled down I was almost on my back.

Ted, the chief drinks-steward, said I could forget the washing-up, and I nodded to him gratefully. I headed towards shanty-town.

And halfway there I discovered I was holding an almost-full bottle of scotch. . . .

I didn't stop to consider the consequences of my action. I undid the metal stopper and threw it away, then lifted the bottle to my lips and swallowed two large mouthfuls.

There was a silent explosion in my throat, and then one in my stomach.

A few minutes later, I fell down and spilt the rest of the scotch. When I stood up, I fell down again. I was sick. I stood up, started laughing . . . and found myself running wildly in the direction of the dormitory hut. Somehow, I never made it. I remember leaning against a wall for a long time, wishing I could find a loo, and then I was walking alone through the darkened camp. A couple passed me, waving and smiling; obviously they

77

recognised me, but didn't realise how drunk I was. After this, I fell down again and tried to get some sleep . . . until I was rudely awakened by two of the security-guards. They lifted me to my feet, and one of them slapped my face. I tried to struggle, thinking they were attacking me. I heard words.

'Who is she?' 'One of the bags . . . I've seen her around.' 'Let's get her up to the huts.' 'Jesus, she's plastered.' I slumped then, and they pulled me roughly to my feet. 'She's got a good pair.' 'Fancy her?' 'Not half.' 'Better leave her alone . . . she's staff.' 'She's pissed.'

I said as clearly as I could: 'What'sh happenenenin' . . . ?'

I couldn't see clearly, though I could feel that one of the men had his arm around me so that it was pressing over my breasts.

'I wanta drink,' I said. 'Gimme one. . . .'

'What do you reckon?' 'Think she'd remember in the morning?' 'She won't remember *anything* in the morning.' 'I've had my eye on this one a long time.' 'OK . . . but let's be quick.'

I felt myself being dragged. I felt grass under my feet, scuffing wetly on my legs where my feet couldn't find a firm purchase on the ground. I felt the men's hands hard on my arms, supporting me, but not allowing me to move either.

'We goin' for a drink?' I said.

'That's right, darling . . . a quick drink.' 'This is gonna be good.' 'These bloody girls, giving it all to the customers.' 'About time we had a bit of it.'

I managed to look round. It was very dark. I couldn't see where we were, it all looked very strange to me.

'This'll do,' one of the men said.

Then I realised through the drunken fog: this was the football field. I was a long way from other people.

And then I knew what was going to happen. . . .

The men released me, and I fell to the ground. One of them stood over me, and pulled my dark-blue jacket from my shoulders. He ripped open my blouse, and snatched at my bra. The cloth resisted, until he pulled again. I felt the strap at the back tear open, and my breasts were free.

I opened my mouth, tried to scream . . . but a hand clamped over me, and I closed my eyes.

My skirt was thrust up over my waist, and I felt rough hands pulling at my pants. I was trying to struggle, but it was no good. I was too weak, too drunk.

When my pants had been torn away, one of the men crouched down beside me. He grabbed my breasts, kneaded them between

78

s fingers. Then he fumbled at the front of his trousers, pulling
em open . . . .

'Who's that?'

I heard the voice, thin and female, calling from the other side
the field.

'Christ . . . there's someone there!'

The man stood up hastily, and backed away. Suddenly, the
her man released his hold on me, and I heard them both running
vay through the grass.

I cried: 'Help. . . .'

'Are you all right?' I heard the girl's voice again, now much
oser. Weakly, I raised myself on my elbows, and saw two
gures running towards me.

'Who is it?' somebody said.

'It's me . . .' I said.

One of the girls flicked a cigarette lighter, and I saw that it was
nn and Di, two of the girls in my hut.

'It's Sally. What's happened love . . .?'

'Two men,' I tried to say, but my tongue wouldn't form the
ords.

For the second time in a few minutes, I felt arms around me . . .
ut now they were gentle and reassuring.

'They . . .'

'It's OK, Sally. They can't hurt you now.'

The other girl said quietly: 'The bastards were going to rape
er. I've been waiting for something like this to happen. Ever
ince Alan left, I've been expecting this.'

'Help me, Di. Let's get her up.'

I was lifted gently, and stood swaying from side to side. My
nees felt very weak, and I looked round helplessly. Ann picked
p the remnants of my clothes, and pulled the torn blouse round
ny shoulders.

'Come on, love. It's not far to the hut.'

The three of us clinging together tightly, we made our way
msteadily to the dormitory hut.

CHAPTER 9

ONE of the girls made an excuse for me, and I took the next day off.

Suddenly the centre of attention, I found that the girls were taking it in turns to sit with me during the day. I stayed the whole time in the hut, not daring to leave.

Of course, I had one hell of a hangover, but in addition the new fact of life about the innocent existence in the camp had really scared me. And scared the other girls too.

'I couldn't see their faces,' I said, again and again. 'It was dark, and I was drunk.'

'It doesn't matter who they were, exactly. It could have been any one of them. It's that Harris's fault. Ever since he arrived, the security guards have been acting like a battalion of Hitler's storm-troops.'

The girl who was sitting with me at that moment was Betty. She had told me that the previous year there had been similar trouble with one of the guards, and when Alan had learnt of it, the man was sacked on the spot.

'So there's nothing we can do. If anything was said to Harris, he wouldn't believe it. And then we'd get another one of his lectures about decent behaviour.'

An hour later, it was Doreen's turn to sit with me. I had been dreading this in a funny kind of way, because I had expected her to truth me about my being drunk. Instead, she was careful to mention it only once.

'If you're going to drink, Sally,' she said, 'then don't drink alone.'

'I'm not drinking any more,' I said.

She shook her head. 'That's stupid. There's nothing wrong with drinking in moderation. But don't go off on any more private benders . . . it's too dangerous.'

'Doreen . . . I'm beginning to think that life at the camp's too dangerous for me anyway.'

She shrugged her shoulders. 'You've been all right until last night. OK, I'll admit that that was a nasty experience, but it isn't likely to happen again. I've been talking to the other girls, and we're getting something sorted out. We'll make sure that after dark there'll always be at least two of us around.'

She saw my expression.

'Listen, Sally . . . this is a *holiday camp*. It's not Harlem. You know the score now, and if we act sensibly nothing will have changed. You're scared to leave the hut now, and that's understandable. But outside the sun is shining, there are eight hundred people enjoying a holiday . . . and you've got a job to do. Take it easy today, but for God's sake don't go getting any hangups about wandering bands of rapists.'

'All I know is,' I said, 'that last night two men tried to rape me.'

'I've told you. It won't – it *can't* – happen again.'

I grinned at her. 'OK, Doreen. If you say so.'

'That's better. Look . . . I've had an idea. I thought you and I might have a bit of fun tonight. All quite harmless, and a good way to get your own back on the male sex.'

'What is it?' I said, suddenly thinking that I didn't quite have a revenge motive against the entire male population of the world.

'That would be telling. Leave it to me. You stay here for the rest of the day, and I'll come and collect you after dinner. Say, about half-past seven. OK?'

I nodded. 'What are you planning, Doreen?'

'You'll see. It's my way of easing you back gently into the big bad world of Priest's Cave Holiday Centre.'

'Hmm . . .' I said doubtfully.

I read a book for a while, then did what I could to repair the damage to my clothes. I managed to sew the bra back into serviceability, and the jacket just had a strained seam. The blouse was beyond repair, and I threw it away. Fortunately, I still had a spare. Then I washed the clothes, had a bath, washed my hair, wrote a letter to Mum and Dad, ironed my clothes, and finished off the book.

I was putting on my dress when Doreen came in.

'You ready?' she said, and then nodded approvingly. 'Good.'

She had a quick wash, changed her clothes and brushed her hair, and then she too was ready.

'Where are we going, Doreen?'

'Oh . . . you'll see.'

She linked her arm in mine, and we set off towards the central complex of camp buildings.

Doreen led me towards one of the bars. It wasn't one of the big ones near the ballroom and night-club, but was in a separate building of its own. It had been designed in the style of a Swiss chalet, and was intended to be a quiet, away-from-it-all corner where the campers could partake of their drinks in isolated surroundings. Instead, the bar had become by unwritten law, one of the few remaining parts of the camp where it was fairly safe to make contacts with the male guests. Tony, the bar-steward cheerfully turned a blind eye to what went on, and went so far as to tip off the girls if he saw one of the security-guards coming.

'Doreen . . .' I said, with a what-the-hell edge to my voice. 'What are you up to?'

'Nothing, Sally. A bit of harmless fun, I promise you.'

'Hmm . . .' I said doubtfully, noticing that there were very few couples in the bar. Most of the clientele appeared to be groups of men.

Doreen took my hand in hers and squeezed it. 'Look, Sally, you don't think I'd let anything happen to you after last night, do you?'

'No, of course not.'

'All right then. Leave the talking to me, and chip in when you've worked out what's going on.'

We walked over to Tony behind the counter.

'Evening Sally. Evening Doreen.'

'Hello, Tony. Two vodkas and lime, please. And don't bother to ring them up, because we don't intend paying for them.'

Tony grinned at her. 'Compliments of the management to you,' he said, pressing the glasses to the optics, and tipping them up with generous splashes of lime. He set them down in front of us, then pulled himself a pint of bitter. 'Cheers.'

'Cheers,' we said, sipping our drinks. Doreen winked at Tony. He winked back.

'Not working tonight?'

'Not on duty, if that's what you mean,' Doreen said. 'How's business here?'

'Can't complain. Slow, but steady.' Tony lowered his voice, and leaned across the bar towards us. 'If it's of any interest to you, your friend Harris was in here just now. Popped his head round the door, and that was that.'

Doreen said: 'Any problems?'

Tony shook his head. 'He won't be back, if that's what you mean.'

'That's what I meant.'

'He's got a regular pattern now. He knows where most of the action is, and makes a point of making a tour every evening. But fortunately for you, he can't be everywhere at once.'

'What about the security-guards?' I said.

'Forget them. They never go into bars where there are guests. They stay in the staff-quarters if they want to drink. That's not entirely through their own choice. Management rule, I believe. The guests don't like the security-guards any more than we do. That's one hangover from Alan Spiers' day that Harris hasn't managed to change.'

Mention of Alan brought an inevitable lurch to my stomach. I took another sip of the vodka, and tried not to think about him.

'But the guards do come round?' I persisted.

'Sure . . . but not until later. They just make sure that everyone's out of the bars at closing-time.'

Just then, a guest walked over to the bar and ordered a round. Tony moved away to serve him. Doreen turned round, and leant against the bar, and I did the same. Suddenly I realised that several of the men were affording us covert glances.

I was slightly embarrassed, and stared fixedly at my drink, but Doreen made capital from their interest. She looked shrewdly at the men, and then nudged me surreptitiously.

'Don't look now,' she whispered, 'but I think I've found our marks.'

Of course, it was impossible for me to resist temptation, and I followed the direction of her gaze. I found myself looking at two very red-faced, nose-peeling male holidaymakers. Middle-aged.

'You've got to be joking,' I said.

'I'm not. I told you . . . we're going to have fun. Those two have obviously come here with their families, and somehow they've managed to get away for a couple of hours. They're kidding themselves they're able to have a whoopee time, and two nubile girls are just what they want. We'll be doing them a favour if we let them buy us a few drinks. They'll want nothing else, simply because they'd be scared stiff if we offered it to them.'

She turned back to face them, and gave them a half-smile. They responded at once; one of them put down his beer-mug so quickly he slopped half of it on the table, and the other climbed awkwardly to his feet.

Doreen grinned at him broadly, and he walked over to us.

'Eh luv, why don't you join us then?'

'Thanks very much,' said Doreen, and knocked back the rest of her vodka. She walked quickly to the table and sat down. Taken by surprise, I gulped the rest of my drink, and followed suit.

The man followed, obviously as much taken aback by our ready response as I was.

'What'll you drink, then?'

'We'll both have a brandy and champagne cocktail,' Doreen said quickly. I nodded.

The man looked worried. 'What about you, Sid?'

'Another pint, please Wilf.'

Wilf walked back to the bar, and Sid – the one who had spilled his drink – stared at us uncomfortably.

'On holiday are you then, love?' he said, and I nearly laughed out loud. Quite a gambit on a holiday-camp.

'No,' I said, struggling to keep a straight face as I caught a glimpse of Doreen's expression. 'I work here, as a matter of fact.'

That seemed to deflate him, and he lapsed into silence until Wilf returned with a trayful of drinks.

'These two lasses work here, Wilf,' said Sid.

'Oh aye? You waitresses, like?'

'Oh no,' said Doreen. 'We work in a special function at the camp. It's hard to describe really, but our job is to make sure the guests are happy. We'll do anything we can to make sure everything runs smoothly.'

Wilf raised an eyebrow, and glanced at Sid.

'Don't seem to have seen you around.'

'Well . . . it's a large camp,' I said.

'Yes, and we're pretty new here,' Doreen said. 'We only started this week. Still finding our way round, if you know what I mean.'

Suddenly, Sid guffawed. 'Oh aye, I know what you mean.'

I realised that Wilf had moved his chair until it was very close to Doreen's, and now he was eyeing her figure whenever he thought she or I wasn't looking.

I felt Sid's arm rest casually on the back of the chair behind me.

'What's your name, darling?' he said to me, in as close an approximation of a husky drawl as I suppose he could manage.

'Er . . . Penny,' I said. 'And this is . . . Dora.'

Doreen glared at me. I disguised a smile.

'Well, Penny and Dora, since it's your job to keep the guests happy, perhaps you can start on us. We're in a celebratory mood tonight, me and Wilf.'

'Oh you're celebrating?' I said. 'What is it, your wedding anniversary or your son's 21st?'

'What makes you think we're married?' said Wilf.

'Well aren't you?' I said.

'We prefer married men,' Doreen put in quickly.

Wilf brightened considerably. His arm too crept round behind.

'Aye, you're right lass. We are married. But me and the wife

84

don't get on too well, y'know. A bit old-fashioned, like.'

Sid nodded, as if to say that went for him too.

Doreen caught my eye, and drank the rest of her cocktail. I followed suit, and banged my glass down very obviously on the table. We both stared at poor Sid.

'Oh . . . Another drink, eh?'

'Same again, please,' I said.

'Bitter for you, Wilf?'

'I'm all right lad. I'll stick with this 'un.'

Sid wandered off to the bar, and came back a moment later with just the two cocktails.

They sat in silence while we sipped them. I kept an eye on Doreen, and decided to match her. She was getting through her drink quickly, and so I finished mine at the same speed.

Sid's enthusiasm appeared to have died a quick death. He was staring glumly at the pool of spilt beer, and every now and then he would glance at his watch. I decided to cheer him up a little, and the next time he looked in my direction I smiled sweetly at him, managing a sexy flutter of eyelashes at the same time. An instant later, I felt his podgey hand sneak round my waist.

'Like another drink, Penny?' he said. 'Or would you girls like to go for a walk, or something?'

'Well. . . .'

'We're not the walking type,' said Doreen quickly. 'And as for "something else", we don't do that until we have a few drinks inside us.'

She laughed suggestively, and I joined in.

'Right,' said Wilf, scraping back his chair noisily. 'What'll it be?'

'Same again, please,' we chorused.

He practically galloped to the bar, and I felt Sid's hand slip slowly down from my waist until it was gripping one of my buttocks in a most unusual way. I didn't care for that, so I shook my body determinedly, and he withdrew. He grinned at me in a sickly sort of way, and instead placed his hand on the top of my leg, just where my skirt ended. I felt his fingers touching my thigh.

At that moment, Wilf came back with two double cocktails, and placed them with ceremony before us.

I leant forward to pick mine up, and as I did so Sid took the opportunity to slide his hand in an upwards direction, raising the hem of my skirt as he did so.

Doreen noticed, and for a moment we glanced at each other. Wilf was taking off his jacket – to reveal two armpits heavily stained with yellow sweat-marks – and was sliding his chair even nearer to Doreen's.

She reached forward for her glass, and seemed to knock it over by accident.

'Oh just look what I've done!' she said. 'Aren't I the clumsy one.'

I noticed that a large part of it had poured over Wilf's trousers. Meanwhile, Sid's hand had pushed back my skirt until even I, from where I was sitting, could see that my panties were being exposed.

'Well, Penny, I think it's time we left.'

'Right on,' I said under my breath. I stood up quickly, and pushed Sid's hand away.

'Aren't you going to finish your drink?' Sid wailed at me, clutching at the last straw of hope as objectionably as he had been clutching at my thighs.

'That's true, Penny,' said Doreen. 'Look . . . it's still untouched.'

I reached over for it, and with all the clumsiness I could muster I tipped it deliberately into his lap.

'Isn't that your wife?' I said to him, pointing towards the door.

'Wha – ?' I couldn't tell whether he was more concerned with the sticky mess in his lap, or the prospect of his old-fashioned wife catching him.

Doreen and I walked away, winking at Tony, who had been watching everything. Outside, we leant against the wall and started laughing.

'That was cruel, Doreen,' I said censuriously.

'Life's cruel. Anyway, you didn't exactly object.'

'I know. But I don't think we should have led them on so far. They can't help being repulsive. We should have left them alone.'

'Maybe you're right.'

We were still outside the bar, and I was feeling anxious that we should move away. I didn't want to be there should Wilf and Sid come out. But before we could move, someone approached.

'Ah . . . Miss Deenes and Miss Brown, is it not?'

'Hello, Mr Harris,' I said, a surge of alarm inside me at the sudden knowledge that had we stayed inside the bar a few moments longer we would have been caught apparently chatting up Wilf and Sid.

'Planning to go inside for a drink?'

'No . . . we're just leaving,' said Doreen. 'It's too crowded in there.'

'Yes. Quite.'

We walked away from him, towards the ballroom. I glanced back once, and saw that he was staring after us.

'There,' said Doreen, 'is a man with one hell of a sex hangup.'

'You think that's what it is?'

'I can't think of any other reason.'

'Do you think we ought to feel sorry for him?'

'There you go again, Sally. That damned nice side of your character coming out just when I'm working up a good, decent hatred. Look, whatever the actual reasons, Harris goes out of his way to make life awkward for a lot of people. You saw a nasty side-result of that last night.'

'You needn't remind me.'

'Sorry.'

We walked on in silence for a while longer.

Then I said: 'What shall we do now?'

'Let's go to another bar. I'm prepared to take my chances with Harris catching us. Let's see if we can find a couple of younger blokes, and have us a good time.'

After the rather seedy incident in the chalet-bar, the prospect seemed attractive.

'OK,' I said.

We went to the camp night-club. It was too early in the evening for the cabaret to have started, but a pianist was tinkling away and the bar was doing a good business. To my relief, there was an about-even distribution of the sexes: several men on their own, several couples, and several girls in groups. There were none of the other girls on the staff there, apart from Chris, who was serving behind the bar.

We bought two drinks – Doreen was back on the vodkas, but I had a bitter lemon – and sat at a table.

'Fancy those two?' Doreen said, nodding towards a table on the other side of the dance-floor.

There were two young men sitting there, doing their best to chat up two very bored-looking girls. Casing the situation as an outside observer, I reckoned that if the men kept plugging away they'd probably make it in the long run, but perhaps they would be in the market for a simpler conquest.

They were quite good-looking: both dressed casually and in fashion, with long hair.

'Not bad,' I said, wishing that Alan were in the camp and I didn't have to be there at all.

'OK. Leave it to me.'

Doreen sat back in her chair, crossed her legs, and waited for one of them to look our way.

When one of them did, she raised her glass to her lips and sipped at it, the while staring at him over the rim.

Two minutes later, he came over to our table and asked her to dance. While they were smooching around the floor together, the second one came over to me . . . and we began dancing too.

Later, at the bar, we discovered that their names were Bob and Eric. Doreen's was Eric, mine was Bob. They were pleasant enough company, and we had a good laugh together. We stayed with them for the rest of the evening, watching the cabaret, dancing between acts and drinking at the bar whenever the occasion presented itself.

And so it was as if in something of a dream that I walked hand in hand with Bob, up through the camp, past row after row of chalets. Doreen and Eric were a few steps in front of us, talking quietly. Suddenly, Eric called Bob over to him, and they talked together softly.

I took the opportunity to have a quick conflab with Doreen.

'What's going on?' I said.

'Don't worry, Sally. You leave everything to me. We're just popping into their chalet to have a drink.'

'OK,' I said weakly, seeing it was easier to go along with her than argue.

Bob strolled back to me, and put his arm around my waist. 'You're coming in for a quick drink then?'

'Yes,' I said.

'Good.'

The two men led us to a chalet, and took us inside. I knew what was going to happen, and it did. There were two single beds there; Doreen and Eric sat down on one, Bob and I on the other. In a moment, Bob was kissing me, and then his hands were reaching for my breasts. My clothes came undone quickly, and soon I was naked. I lay back on the bed, watching him undress, his body silhouetted against the faint light coming in through the curtained window. In the other bed, I could tell by the sounds that Doreen and Eric were already well on the job.

Bob lay down beside me, and a few seconds later he entered me. I closed my eyes, allowing my body to enjoy itself, while cutting my mind off from what I was doing.

I think I must have fallen asleep afterwards, for the next thing I was aware of was Doreen shaking my shoulder.

'Come on Sally, get dressed. We'd better get back to shanty-own. We're on first shift in the morning.'

I disentangled myself from Bob's arms, and stood up. He was well asleep. Doreen was already dressed, and she helped me find my clothes. We let ourselves out of the chalet. Behind us, one of the men was snoring.

As we walked through the dark and now silent camp, Doreen grabbed hold of my hand and pressed something crisp into it.

'Here,' she said. 'I owe you fifty pence.'

'What's this? I said, feeling that there were two pound-notes in my hand.

'That's your share. I only asked them for a fiver.'

The implication of it didn't sink in at first. But in the next few minutes, as we walked on up the hill towards the dormitory hut, the awful realisation came that the money was for services rendered. I'd walked into it blithely, and in full awareness of what I was doing. But those two pound notes, resting in my hand, confirmed that at last I had joined Doreen and her friends.

Perhaps all along it had only been a question of time.

CHAPTER 10

SHOCK has a way of setting in slowly. The next morning, which being a Friday was a busy one, I hardly had time to think, let alone react to my new realisation.

I was in double-shock, if a mild form. Partly because of Alan, and partly because of what I had done the night before.

Alan's absence had led – directly or indirectly – to my recent behaviour. I wanted him, needed him. But he was unobtainable and unattainable. And so I had drifted into a wanton existence.

But it was that which horrified me so.

For most of the morning I slaved away, full of gay smiles and friendly help to the happy holidaymakers. After the breakfast shift, the children's treasure hunt. After that, bingo. After that, blowing a whistle to start the swimming-races. After that, lunch.

On Fridays we were not allowed any time off officially, because it was the day into which was packed as much entertainment for the guests as possible. Nevertheless, there was a long-standing agreement with the management that we could take it in turns to have an hour off here and there if we could find someone to stand in for us. I had a quiet word with Doreen, and we agreed to double up for each other so that we could both have an hour off. As soon as the lunch-shift was out of the way, Doreen sped off to the tennis-courts to stand in for me, and I walked slowly up to the landscaped gardens which had been designed as the 'quiet' corner of the camp.

As usual, there were mostly old-age pensioners here, nodding away in the sun. They ignored me, and I walked until I found an unoccupied bench.

I don't remember coming to any conscious decision during that hour. I just sat there in the sun with my eyes closed, listening to the noises in the distance from the people enjoying themselves. The only positive thinking I did was about something Alan had once said. 'You're only here because you're trying to escape from something.' True enough, but what I had escaped into was something now from which I wanted to get away. Alan had become my sole reason for staying here. The camp was a bright artificial existence, totally divorced from reality. But reality had a nasty way of making itself felt. Like . . . selling one's body.

I still had the two pounds, rolled up into a thin cylinder which I rubbed continually between the palms of my hands. I didn't consider what to do with it; as I said, I made no conscious decision.

But when my watch said my hour was up, I walked down to the tennis-courts by way of the camp shop, and quietly slipped the two notes into a collecting box for spastic children.

I didn't want the money, and it may as well go somewhere useful.

When I saw Doreen, she gave me the fifty pence she 'owed' me; that too found its way into the box.

It didn't change the principle of what I had done, any more than Lady Macbeth wringing her hands, but at least I had made the symbolic gesture. Which, on that sunny but dark day, was at least something.

For the next few days I coasted. The job continued, and that was the easiest part of the existence. Whatever my internal feelings, I still got a certain amount of pleasure from helping the campers enjoy themselves.

It was silly really. I had very little to do, apart from look pretty and happy, and help out with the actual behind-the-scene organising. And yet it was still possible to get more than a small

ck out of people coming up to me at the end of their stay and
anking me for making it such a success for them.

Now, though, I was keeping clear of the bottle, and whenever
oreen suggested she and I might have some 'fun,' I always
scovered a letter I had to write, or some clothes to wash.

As near as possible, I was back to the Sally that had existed
efore Alan had left.

But I was different in one respect. I had made a decision that I
ould leave the camp, and go back home. I'd had enough.

I had already been paid up until the end of that week, and I
ecided that would be the best time to leave. I didn't intend going
o see Mr Harris to hand in my notice. I'd simply leave on the
aturday morning, and lose myself amongst the homegoing
olidaymakers. Payday for the staff was the Saturday (paid in
dvance for the week coming), and if I didn't turn up to collect
y pay-packet, they'd realise soon enough.

In a sense, I was following Alan's example. Just up and go. . . .

The decision made, I felt myself growing more objective about
he camp. I was in it, but not of it.

This tawdry world of escape was no such thing; it was just
nother way of living a life. I wanted no more of it.

The Monday passed, and then the Tuesday.

I was on duty on the Tuesday evening, serving behind the bar
n the ballroom. It had been a moderate night, though earlier on a
roup of men had been indulging in some hard drinking.

I was washing glasses behind the bar with Daph, when Doreen
ushed in.

'Give me a drink, Sally, there's a love.'

I stared at her. I had never seen her like this before. Her face
vas pale, and her hair was untidy. Even the provocative curves
f her figure seemed to have receded.

'What's the matter, Doreen?'

'Nothing. Come on, love, give me a drink.'

I poured her a vodka, and she took it from me, emptying the
glass in one. Daph and I exchanged glances.

'That's better.'

'All right . . . now will you tell us?'

'It was terrible, Sally. There's been a fight.'

'A fight? Where?'

'Behind some of the chalets. I was . . . walking that way, and I
aw it happen.'

Daph said: 'Who was involved?'

'I don't know,' said Doreen, shaking her head. 'A group of the campers. They were drunk. They were being beaten up by the guards.'

'*What*?'

She nodded firmly. 'That's what I saw. There were four men and about six of the guards.'

She sat down suddenly on one of the bar-stools. She lit a cigarette, and I poured her another drink, paying for it with my own money.

'But was anyone hurt?'

'I think so. Two of the men were lying on the ground, and the others ran away. God, Sally . . . it was *terrible*. It was all so quiet, no shouting or anything. As if they were in deadly earnest. Every time they kicked them, there was this horrible thudding sound . . . but apart from that it was silent. . . .'

She burst into tears. I had never seen her so upset, and in that moment I saw that beneath her hard and painted exterior Doreen was just as capable of reacting to an emotional situation as anyone.

Daph and I finished clearing up, and we locked up the bar for the night. The three of us walked together up to the dormitory-hut, scared stiff that we might run into some of the guards. But the camp was still, like a town under curfew. It was almost as if everyone there knew what had happened, and was staying out of sight until the trouble blew over.

The next morning, the camp appeared to be back to normal. The sun was shining, people milled around in the holiday clothes, and sweet music played as usual over the speakers. It took on the dimensions of an awful dream in the night.

During the morning we heard both sides of the story through the grapevine. Fortunately, most of the campers hadn't heard anything about the trouble, and were unaffected by it. But one or two of the girls heard about the fight from some of the male guests, and of course the security-guards' side of the story trickled through to us.

There was a conflict of truth, of course, but through hearing both sides of the story, we were able to piece together some kind of factual version.

Apparently, it had started on the Monday night. One of the male guests had come with his fiancée, and as the camp wouldn't allow unmarried couples the luxury of sharing a chalet they'd had to take two singles. The man had gone to the girl's chalet when she went to bed, and was caught leaving it in the early hours of the morning.

The guard had been officious, and the guest had struck him in a moment of anger. As a result, the guard had called one of his buddies, and given the guest what was – by the next night's standard – a mild thrashing.

OK, both were wrong: the guard shouldn't have been officious, and the guest shouldn't have struck him. One all.

But on the Tuesday, the guest had got together with several of his mates and planned some revenge.

They waited in the shadows until two security-guards came by, then attacked. Unfortunately for them, they didn't know that the guards were expecting this, and had reinforcements nearby. Outnumbered, the four guests had been badly roughed up.

In the afternoon, I saw the four men, sitting together in moody silence beside the entrance to one of the bars. All of them had bad bruising on the face, two had cut lips and one of them had a bandage round his head.

I don't like violence, and I had no brief for either side, so in a sense I was an outside observer. But it brought home one unpleasant fact: that the situation regarding the security-guards had grown distinctly worse. I tried to remember back to the days when Alan had been in charge of the staff . . . and found that I was hardly aware of the guards. If I hadn't been told about them, I doubt if I would have even suspected their existence.

But now, with Harris keeping the staff in firm control, the guards seemed to be everywhere. And the frightening thing was that they were by and large the same men. It was a clear demonstration of the way people's behaviour could be changed. Doubtless, Harris treated the guards to long pep-talks about his own brand of morality, and promised them his support in seeing it was carried out. Perhaps he was even able to arrange discreet bonuses or perks.

In any event, the incident with the fight, and what had happened to me, made almost the whole staff – certainly the stewardettes – aware that there was now an unofficial police-force in the camp. And not one bound by Home Office regulations.

Nor, it seemed, by holiday camp regulations. As far as I know, none of the guards was reprimanded for his involvement in the scuffle.

It just made me more glad that I had decided to leave. I had a couple of hours off in the afternoon, and went to the pool with Betty. As we lay there sunbathing, I saw two of the guards come down to the pool. They too were off-duty, and were dressed in swimming-trunks . . . but immediately the whole atmosphere seemed to change.

In a while, Betty and I could stand it no longer, and we went back to the dormitory hut to change.

The Wednesday passed without incident . . . unless you call one of the teenage girls being thrown into the swimming-pool at midnight an incident.

Then on the Thursday, as I was serving breakfasts, Jimmy got up on the rostrum for the usual morning announcements . . . and said something that stopped me dead in my tracks.

'. . . Tonight we have a cartoon-show for all the kiddies. Seven o'clock in the ballroom, we have Tom and Jerry, Sylvester, Donald Duck and all the favourites. Mum and Dad can have an hour or so of freedom . . . so why not find yourself a corner in one of our bars? But don't stay too long, folks, because when the film-show's over and we've cleared away the chairs, the ballroom's all yours for Olde Time Dancing. You must know everybody by now, so come along and have a good time.

'For those of you who don't fancy that . . . well, we've really got something special lined up for you.

'Thursday night is beat night in the discotheque, and we have a live group performing for you. Not, as it says in your camp-programme, the Panthers . . . unfortunately, the drummer has been taken ill and they've had to cancel. Instead . . . well, we've gone to town and we've managed to obtain a group who are currently at number 3 in the charts. They're coming down specially from London to play for us tonight.'

I had stopped dead in my tracks. Around me, the whole restaurant seemed to have frozen into immobility.

Maxima Culpa, I said urgently. *It's Maxima Culpa. Maxima Culpa.*

'They're a local band who've managed to break in to the big time, and I know' (*Maxima Culpa Maxima Culpa*) 'you'll give them all your support. They're called Ess Pry, and they'll be starting their gig at . . . '

I wasn't listening any more.

Ess Pry? Who in hell were Ess Pry?

The disappointment welled in me like a physical presence. Of course, it had been too much of a fantastic chance that it would be Maxima Culpa, and to have built up my hopes, even in those few seconds, was ridiculous. I walked out of the restaurant in a daze, and dumped some plates for washing by the hatch.

Afterwards, the faint hope that Jimmy's words had stirred in

94

he flickered to life again. Hadn't he said that they were a local
roup who'd made good? Perhaps it was Alan and the others,
under a new name . . .

I asked Doreen about it.

'You heard about that group who're playing tonight?'

'No. Who are they?'

'Ess Pry.'

'S What?'

'Ess Pry,' I repeated.

'Never heard of them. Are they any good?'

'That's what I was hoping you'd tell me.'

'Why . . . are you thinking of going?'

'I don't know yet.'

As soon as I could find her, I spoke to Sarah, one of the other
stewardettes. She always had Radio One on, and I thought if
anyone would know anything about them she would.

'Ess Pry,' she said. 'Oh they're fantastic. They're on tonight.'

'I know. But I was wondering if you knew anything about
them.'

'Not really. They come from somewhere round here, though.
Somewhere in Devon.'

'Did they ever play under any other name?'

Sarah frowned. 'I don't think so. At least, I've never heard of
it if they did. Here, they're at number 1 at the moment.'

'Number 3,' I said in a hollow voice.

Sarah stared after me with a puzzled expression as I walked
away.

I wouldn't settle until I knew for certain, so I sought out Don,
the pianist, once again. He lent me his trade paper, and I took it
into a quiet corner to read at leisure.

Sure enough, Ess Pry were mentioned. There was even a
photograph of them.

They were a Devon group, who'd started out in the Torbay
area. They'd started out as Ess Pry, and they stayed that way.
They'd had a couple of hit records already, and were currently
packing them in all over the country. They played hard rock and
roll, and attracted a violent element in their audiences which kept
concert-hall managers on their toes.

I stared at the photograph for a good five minutes.

Alan was not – emphatically not – a member of the group. The
flicker of hope was well and truly extinguished.

Well, I thought to myself, if Ess Pry like playing to violent
audiences, they're coming to the right place.

At any other time, such a maudlin thought would have alarmed me with its spontaneity, but now I was past caring. Two more nights in the camp, and I would be finished with it forever.

I took the paper back to Don, and thanked him.

'You thinking of taking up a musical career?' he said.

'No. Why?'

'You seem very interested in what's going on.'

'Oh . . . I just know someone who plays in a group. I like to find out what he's up to. Are you going to watch this pop-group tonight?'

Don laughed. 'Not likely! I'll be doing my barn-dance thing in the ballroom.'

'Oh yes. Of course.'

My interest in Ess Pry died as quickly as it had been born. Now I knew they were nothing to do with Alan they might have been, for all I cared, the original group who'd had to cancel.

I hurried away, and joined Betty at the coffee-shop. Every morning, from ten until half-past eleven, coffee and buns were sold in a little bar behind the swimming-pool. It was one of the most relaxing parts of the camp, and I enjoyed working there.

The day passed smoothly, marred at only one point by a glimpse I caught of one of the off-duty guards, standing in the distance and watching the swimmers with a scowl.

Two more nights, I thought again, and all this will be behind me. Doreen, security-guards, Harris . . . everything.

I couldn't have known at that point that I had already spent my last night in the camp.

CHAPTER 11

THERE was a feeling of anticipation in the camp, quite unlike anything I had experienced there before. While I was serving on the dinner shift I could detect it, and afterwards in one of the bars the same feeling was there.

My work for the day finished at eight, and at about five past I left the bar and started walking up towards the dormitory-hut. I was intending to have a bath and wash my hair, read a book and then have an early night.

On the way, I saw two of the men who had been involved in the fight with the guards. They took no notice of me, talking quietly to each other. But I noticed that each was wearing a large round badge on his lapel, and as they passed I saw what was written on it.

Diagonally across the centre was a large wooden club with a nail hammered through the end. Across the top was written: E S S, and across the bottom: P R Y.

Then I saw a group of teenage girls, walking down towards the discotheque, carrying a banner which they'd evidently just made: ESS PRY WE LUV YOU.

I was amazed how out of touch I had become while I was at the camp. Ess Pry were obviously well known and very popular. It was then that I recognised the feeling of anticipation in the camp. Quite simply, the management either by fluke or good judgement had hired a group for the night that everyone wanted to see. Holiday camps attract a large number of young people, and evidently Ess Pry were one of the biggest groups of the moment.

A small piece of the outside world was coming to the camp, and the younger guests appreciated it.

It made me wonder, as I walked on up to the hut, if a clue lay here to the future of camps. Perhaps it was only the family type of guests who wanted to escape from the outside for a few days; the young people went on holiday too, but it wasn't escape they were seeking. Give them a bit of what they were familiar with, and they loved it.

Just as I was going through the door of the hut, Daph came out.

'Hi, Sally.'

'Hi.'

I stared at her. She was wearing faded denim jeans, and a skimpy armless tee-shirt with no bra underneath.

'Where are you going?'

'Down to the disco, of course. Aren't you going?'

'I wasn't planning to.'

'Then you must be just about the only person in the camp under 25 who isn't.'

'You're going to see the group?'

'Of course. My God, this is the first thing that's happened at the camp that's worth doing.'

'Are they that good then?'

She looked at me as if I was half out of my mind.

'Sally . . . they're fantastic. Come on . . . you'll enjoy yourself.'

'OK,' I said. 'I'll be down later. I've got to change first.'

'Good. I'll see you there. But don't be long. If you're there much after half-past you won't get in.'

'I'll be there,' I said.

She grinned at me, and hurried on down towards the central complex of buildings.

Once inside the hut, I found I was alone. Everyone else appeared to be either on duty or already down at the discotheque.

Now . . . I've always been a bit of a procrastinator. I can only hurry if there's someone there to egg me on. Left to myself, I dawdle around, pottering about with make-up and hairbrushes and things. And this is what happened. Without Daph's evident enthusiasm I moved around slowly. I skipped the bath, and had a strip-wash instead. I left my hair, and gave it a good brushing. And then I spent about ten minutes trying to decide which clothes to wear. In the end I decided to do as Daph had done, and slipped on my oldest pair of jeans and a tee-shirt. Like Daph, too, I left off my bra.

But with all this time wasted, I didn't get down to the discotheque until after a quarter to nine.

I took one look through the door, and changed my mind about going inside. It was jammed solid with people, and music was being played loudly through speakers to the waiting audience.

I asked one of the bar-stewards, who was acting as doorman for the evening, what time the group started.

'About half-past nine, I think.'

I decided I'd wait outside. In spite of Daph's warning, I felt confident of being able to get it later. I was on the staff, wasn't I?

It was a warm evening, so I decided to walk around by myself for a bit. In the last few weeks, I had grown used to being on my own; if not physically alone – it's impossible to find solitude in a camp – then certainly alone mentally.

At the back of the discotheque I came across the group's band-wagon. Over the front was a vividly-painted slogan: ESS PRY – PURVEYORS OF ROCK TO THE WORLD. All over its sides, back and – for all I knew – its roof, people had scrawled slogans. Some were written with a finger in the dirt, others were in lipstick and a few were more indelibly penned with a knife in the paint. They were the typical fan-messages to the group: *Ess Pry We Luv You*, *MikeMikeMike*, *Screw Me* . . . and dozens of others. One girl (I presume) had scrawled her vital statistics and a phone-number.

A roadie was sitting in the back, smoking a cigarette and fiddling with a piece of electronic equipment. He grinned at me.

I walked away from the discotheque, in the direction of the ballroom. From inside, I heard the melody of *Smoke Gets in Your Eyes*, and over this the sound of voices. I walked round the swimming-pool, seeing the water still and dark in the evening. Two men passed me, and they noticed my figure showing obviously through my tee-shirt. As they went in the direction of the ballroom, one said something to the other and they both wheezed with laughter.

And then Mr Harris was there.

'Good evening, Miss Deenes.'

'Hullo.'

I couldn't think of anyone I wanted to meet less. I looked at him expressionlessly, and moved to walk past him.

'Not on duty this evening?'

'No.'

'Are you going to the dance?'

'In there?' I nodded towards the ballroom.

'Yes. A very enjoyable evening, I should say. I like dancing myself. Do you like dancing, Miss Deenes?'

'No.'

'I hope you're not thinking of going to the discotheque. I don't know what got into the entertainments committee when they hired that group. They have a disgusting reputation, did you know?'

'No, I didn't.'

'Well if you'll take my advice, you'll stay well away from there this evening. My men will make sure things don't get out of hand, but even so I find the whole thing unsavoury.'

It was at that precise moment that I decided I would be spending the rest of the evening watching Ess Pry.

I moved round him.

'Excuse me, Mr Harris, but I'm on my way up to the hut.'

'Good girl. Best place to be this evening.'

I walked past him without another word. When I reached the line of trees at the edge of the patio by the pool, I turned round. Harris was speaking to one of his security-guards. After a moment, they both went together into the ballroom.

I headed for the discotheque.

I could feel the bass-notes of the music throbbing through the ground, even when I was still fifty yards from the discotheque.

At first I thought the group had started playing, but then recognised the number as a track from a Faces album. Ess Pry had not yet started.

I walked on.

And then . . . from the direction of the camp gates I heard the sound of engines. . . .

The noise grew rapidly, and looking in that direction I saw the glare of headlights. I stopped, and watched curiously.

The noise grew louder, until it was deafening . . . and then the motorbikes were roaring past me.

Although it was not yet completely dark, the discotheque had been built in a shallow hollow and the surroundings were gloomy. I could not see the riders as they circled past me, only the black silhouettes of their shapes. Some of the bikes had one rider, and others had two. In the customary quiet of the camp – where the only noises were generally music or voices – the shattering sound of the unsilenced exhausts was exhilarating. So too was the smell, which brought back memories of the one and only time I had ever been to the speedway.

I was merely a spectator; the riders were taking no notice of me. They circled round where I stood, and brought their bikes to a stop in an untidy group a few yards from the entrance to the discotheque. From the doorway, the steward looked at them anxiously.

Engines stopped, riders levered themselves up in their seats, and grimy goggles were lifted away to reveal greasy faces.

For a moment, they stayed on their machines. I looked at them, suddenly realising that I was seeing a complete chapter of Hell's Angels. I had never been this close before, and my first instinct was one of fear.

What were they doing here? What did they want?

I had heard terrible stories about the Angels. Wherever they went, they threatened peace and quiet, bringing their own form of rough justice and violent actions with them. They certainly looked threatening enough.

The only thing about them that was clean and efficient-looking was the condition of their bikes. Every single one had been polished with loving care, and shone as if it were new. Extravagant badges and flags decorated the sides and handlebars, and where the machine was styled with chromium it reflected the coloured lights by the discotheque like a new mirror.

But the Angels themselves were as filthy and animalistic in their appearance as their machines were slick and precision-engineered.

There was not one who looked as if he had washed in the last year. Or shaved. Or changed his clothes. There was not one who looked as if he had ever worn anything other than faded jeans, roll-top boots, leather jacket encrusted with studs and colours, dirty rag around his throat, battered helmet on his head. There was not one who . . . no, there was one.

One of the Angels had stopped his bike at ninety degrees to the others, and sat upright on the leather seat. He regarded the others at first, then turned and looked through the entrance of the discotheque. Evidently satisfied that this was the right place, he nodded. The others dismounted, and shambled in an arrogant mob through the doorway. I saw the steward pressed back as if he had not stood there at all.

But this one, whom the others so obviously followed, was different. Or so he appeared to me.

Like the others, his hair was long, greasy and hung around his face in tangled knots. He wore the obligatory uniform of denim and leather. A nazi Iron Cross dangled at his throat, and a swastika was stencilled on each of the arms of his jacket.

I felt, though, that he was different. I could see his face in the light from the doorway, and it seemed aware, perhaps slightly amused. His face was clean-shaven, and his boots were polished. The studs on his jacket were not dulled by weather, but polished so that they glowed.

And he seemed in no hurry to join the others. They, and their girlfriend 'mommas', had disappeared into the club, and now I stood alone with this Angel . . . and the fear in me had vanished.

He saw me there, as if for the first time. Casually, he swung his legs off the machine and walked towards me.

'This the right place for Ess Pry?' he said.

I nodded, and said nothing.

'What's the matter? You not scared?'

I shook my head. 'No.'

'Don't you worry about the others. They do what I say. If I say you're all right, they won't look at you.' He scowled round at the camp . . . or at least, the part of it that was visible from where we stood. 'What is this place?'

'It's a holiday camp.'

'Oh yeah.' He sounded totally uninterested. 'You want a ride on my bike?'

'Er . . . no thanks.'

'What's the matter, don't you like the bike?'

He glanced at it proudly. I walked over to it quickly, and did a quick appraisal of it. Obviously, it was the most important thing in his life.

'It's fantastic,' I said tactfully. 'I've never seen anything like it in my life.'

'OK . . . you want a ride?'

'I wanted to . . . go and watch the group.'

He shrugged. 'OK. That's what I came for.'

He took my hand in his paw, and walked me quickly towards the club.

I said: 'Listen . . . you can't go in there.'

'An' who's gonna stop me?'

'Well it's private property.'

He grinned broadly. 'Listen, chick, there ain't any such thing. I'm Slippery Hick, and me and my Angels go where we like. You get?'

'OK. It's not my problem.'

Unexpectedly, he laughed out loud.

'Is that really your name? Slippery Hick, I mean.'

'What's wrong with it?'

'Nothing's wrong with it. I just wondered.'

'Yeah, it's my name. But you can call me Hick. What do they call you?'

'Sally.'

'I call you Sal . . . right?'

'Right.'

'You're a good chick, Sal. Listen, you want a ride on my bike after the music?'

'Maybe.'

At that moment we went in through the door, and suddenly the music was too loud to speak over.

Inside, the room was packed solid . . . the numbers distinctly swelled by the Hell's Angels and their mommas. I noticed that most of them had shouldered their way through to the front, and several had produced cans of beer which they were swilling back with disconcerting speed.

Hick led me through the crowd, until we were near the front ourselves. The stage was still empty of performers, but there were several large amplifiers and speakers waiting, and a drum-kit. Two roadies were adjusting the equipment, and as I watched one of them tested the P.A. system by clicking his fingers in front of the mikes. The sound came through the speakers like a minia-ture explosion, that deadened for an instant the music that was being played from a record.

In a while, the record finished and a man's voice came over the system.

'In a moment we have for you a group from London . . . Ess Pry.' Several people cheered, and the Angels roared hoarsely and stamped their boots. 'But first I must remind everyone here that this is a private holiday camp, and is open only to guests staying here. Would all others kindly leave, please.'

This was a clear reference to Hick and his friends, but for all the notice they took nothing need have been said. An Angel near me swallowed some beer, then belched loudly.

'Ladies and gentlemen . . . Ess Spry!'

To a riot of cheering, five young men walked on stage, raising their hands in acknowledgement. I stared at them in absolute fascination. I'd seen some dirty, depraved-looking groups in my time . . . but this lot took some beating. In comparison, they managed to make the Angels look like well-heeled gents about town.

They picked up their guitars, and one sat at an organ, the other at the drums.

One of the guitarists stepped forward to the microphone.

'OK folks. We got some rock for you tonight. One . . . two . . . three . . . four. . . .'

On the fourth beat, they started. A veritable explosion of noise seemed to crash out from the stage, the blast feeling as if it was going to crush my chest. I half stepped back in reaction, and found myself pressing up against the person behind. I glanced up at Hick . . . but he was taking no notice of me. His eyes were closed, his head was going back and forward in time with the beat. And the beat. . . . It was like nothing I'd ever experienced. The strongest, heaviest, dirtiest rock beat I'd ever heard in my life. The drums and bass-guitar throbbed out the underlying rhythm, the guitars played riffs, and the organ wailed out a harsh scream of sound. Within seconds of them starting, I could feel that everyone in the room was directly responding to the sound.

This was rock from the core. No frills, no pretentions. In direct line of descent from Little Richard, Larry Williams and other rock stars of the fifties, this was rock-music from the seventies. Louder, deeper and a whole world earthier, I saw at once why Ess Pry appealed to the primaeval instinct in audiences.

At first I was alienated by the music. It was not being played for my enjoyment; rather, it was as if it was being thrown at me.

The whole stance of the group was one of aggression and despite. I was frightened by the music, intimidated by it. I felt I had to get away before it killed me, or somehow altered me in some ineradicable way. But then it began to reach me, insidiously working its way into my soul . . . and I found my body moving in time with the music, my feet stamping out the rhythm on the floor.

As the first number ended, there was a roar of applause. The Angels in particular were wholly appreciative.

As the group made minor adjustments to their equipment, I found myself looking around. And there, at the side of the stage, I saw something that alarmed me more than the music – for all its inherent aggression – had done.

There were two of the security-guards there, and they were watching the Angels. Even as I looked, one appeared to be counting them. He spoke to the other, and they both nodded. Then one left the discotheque by a side door.

Fear welled in me. I had an awful suspicion of what was to come. . . .

I slipped away from Hick's side, and squeezed my way back through the crowd. I was only halfway through as Ess Pry launched into their second number: a slow rhythm-and-blues, which throbbed insistently and repetitively while one of the group blew deafeningly through an amplified harmonica.

I made it to the door, and walked out into the cool night. Behind me, the sound of the music diminished slightly, but even so it was still loud enough, I felt sure, to be heard over half the camp.

I moved sideways, and stood in the shadows beside the doorway. I had already seen what I had suspected. . . .

Harris was there, and with him stood virtually the entire security staff. The man I had seen leave the discotheque joined the group, and spoke to Harris. The man nodded, and spoke to the others. He pointed . . . first towards the discotheque, then secondly at the group of motorcycles. More nodding, more instructions.

Quite apart from the deliberate way in which they were planning their attack – for that was no more or less than what it was – the thing that disturbed me most was that each of the security-guards was wearing a motor-cycle crash-helmet.

And those who weren't carrying clubs of wood, were gripping large spanners or wrenches. . . .

Harris didn't want the Angels here on his camp, and he was

determined to throw them out. By force.

I had no loyalty to the Angels, but then that was equally true of my feelings towards Harris. And anyway, what had the Angels done? By their standards, nothing. They were listening to music. There had been no trouble, no provocation. They'd simply arrived and, if my guess was correct, would simply leave when the concert was finished.

I darted back into the heat, noise and crush of the discotheque.

I wormed my way furiously through the crowd, trying to find Hick. He was standing where I had left him, rocking backwards and forwards on the heels of his boots, in time with the music.

I grabbed his arm, and tugged it frantically. He grinned down at me, probably unaware even that I had left his side for a few moments.

I shouted at him: 'Outside! Trouble!'

It was ridiculous to try. The music was just too loud. Hick grinned at me again, and turned back to face the music. I waited impatiently for the number to finish . . . but as is the way of blues it seemed to go on for an eternity.

In the end, though, it had to finish, and as the crowd roared with applause I tugged at Hick's arm again.

'Hi, Sal. Ain't they great?'

'Hick! There's a crowd of men outside, looking for trouble!'

He shrugged. 'Let 'em.'

'But they're after *you*!'

'So what? They know where we are.'

I almost screamed with frustration. 'Don't you understand . . . they're going to smash your bikes?!'

Hick moved.

He barrelled his way through the crowd, snatching at the arms of the other Angels.

'Rumble! Get 'em! *Rumble*!'

In seconds the whole group of Angels was mobilised. They barged their way to the door, knocking people aside. Hick was in the lead.

As he ran through the door, one of the guards was waiting for him and a club swung from the shadows and knocked him to the ground.

By the time I managed to get outside, a full fight was in progress. It was a mean, dirty fight, obeying no rules at all.

The guards used their clubs, and they aimed at the Angels' guts and necks. The Angels drew heavy chains from their pockets, smashed the necks from bottles, and used anything they could lay their hands on.

Hick was not badly hurt. The first blow had caught him on the side of his head, but the steel helmet he wore protected him from the worst. Blood trickled down his face, and once he had regained his feet he pitched into the fight with no less vigour than any of the others.

Many people were screaming, and a crowd was gathering rapidly. I saw three of the guards move in concert on the pile of bikes, raising their steel wrenches to smash at the metal. The Angels saw this, and moved to protect their beloved machines. The guards fell, and no more attempt was made to damage the machines.

In less than a minute, it was clear the Angels were winning. They were fewer in number, but obviously they were accustomed to fighting dirty. Two or three of the guards who fell were helped away, and several more ran off.

It was over quickly. After the first few seconds, in which it was never clear who could possibly come out unharmed, the Angels showed their prowess as dirty scrappers and the guards never stood a chance.

Bloody and bruised, but without any real injury, the Angels stood panting as the guards backed off.

'You bitch! I saw you . . . you warned them!'

I turned, and saw that Harris was standing near me. He had obviously not taken part personally in the fight, but had witnessed everything.

'That's right. I warned them.'

'Well just you wait. The police will be here in a moment, and that'll be the end of you.'

Even as he spoke, the sound of sirens could be heard in the distance.

I turned back on Harris, and walked over to Hick. Like the other Angels, he was climbing on to his machine.

I said: 'You'd better go. The fuzz are coming.'

In the background, a motorcycle was kicked into life. Then another . . . and soon they'd all started their engines.

Over the racket, Hick said: 'You did us a favour, Sal. You want that ride on my bike?'

I turned once more, and saw Harris watching me. Quite deliberately, I raised two fingers at him.

'Yes, please.'

I climbed on to the pillion, and held on tight. In the distance, beyond the trees that fringed the camp, I could see the bright blue flash of the police car's light.

Hick jumped on the kick-start, and the engine roared loudly. He let in the clutch at once, and we shot away. I thought at first that he and the Angels were going to make a run for it . . . but no, he turned away from the main drive, and hurtled over the grass and through some trees, where the police car could not follow. Behind us, the other Angels followed.

We roared through the camp, skidding round the chalets, bumping over the uneven ground. At one point a group of men tried to stop us, but Hick just held the throttle open and the Angels shot through the gap that was hurriedly made.

Sitting where I was, holding on to Hick's body for dear life, I hardly saw the camp whizzing past. But even in the excitement of the moment I realised I was probably seeing the place for the last time.

Hick hit a bump, and for a moment I thought I was seeing everything for the last time . . . but then he righted the machine expertly, swung it on to one of the tarmacadam paths and accelerated through the children's playground, down a slope, past the restaurant, and out to the discotheque.

Three police-cars stood there, and several policemen were interviewing the crowds of people. We were through and past them before they even had time to register our presence . . . and then we were on the main road.

Hick glanced behind him to see if the other Angels were still with us, and then he turned the throttle and the machine seemed to leap forward.

The road lay ahead of us, smooth and black. Beneath my legs the engine growled faster and faster, and soon I had to narrow my eyes against the violent slipstream. Hick was hunched over the handlebars, his hair whipping back from under his helmet and flapping against my cheeks. Behind us I could hear the racket of the other Angels, matching Hick's speed.

Just once, I levered myself up far enough to see the speedometer. At that point, the needle was hitting 80, and still rising. I hunched down, clutched Hick tighter and closed my eyes. I had no time, no breath, no spare mental energy to consider what I was doing. All I knew was that I had left the camp for ever.

The road lay in a straight line across the moors to the west of the town. To my right lay the sea, to my left the dark country-side.

And Hick went on accelerating as if there was no limit to the speed his machine could reach.

CHAPTER 12

I AWOKE on the beach. Hick lay next to me, covered with a blanket. We had slept together on the sand, but we had not made love. He had tried, and I had refused him. To my surprise he had not persisted, and eventually we had fallen asleep lying chastely by each other's side.

In the morning, I helped the other Angel girls heat up some meat from some cans; that, and a few tins of beer, was all the breakfast we had.

I was concerned for the Angel's injuries, but much to my surprise they carried their bruises and cuts like medals honourably awarded. Hick himself had a nasty gash under his hair, and the side of his face was matted with dried blood, but when I offered to wash it off he just grinned and opened another can of beer.

There were eighteen Angels in the chapter, and twelve of them had mommas. I didn't talk much to the other girls. I tried to make conversation, but they seemed disinterested. I think they were wrapped up entirely in their world of speed, beer and bikes.

In the cold reality of that morning, I realised that I was totally at the mercy of the Angels. I had no money, no possessions . . . no change of clothes even.

'Don'tcha worry, Sal,' Hick said as he ate the warmed-up meat. 'You'll be all right with us.'

To prove his point, he and three other Angels 'escorted' me into a nearby village where he bought me a postcard and a stamp . . . then lent me a pen to write with.

I sent the card to Doreen, at the camp. I told her I was all right, and asked her to find all my belongings and send them back to Mum and Dad, using the money which was in my purse. I knew I could trust her to do this for me.

Back at the beach, I asked Hick what we were doing.

'Waitin' . . .' he said, and explained no more.

We hung around all day. None of the Angels ever seemed to wash, so when I went down to the edge of the sea I was by myself. I stripped off all my clothes, and plunged into the water. The day was hot, so afterwards I just lay on the sand in the nude until I was dry, then got dressed again and went back to the others.

'What are we doing now?' I said.

'Waitin'. . . .'

I was beginning to wonder how long they intended waiting, because as far as I could see they had no food, and only a few more cans of beer. It didn't seem to worry them at all; in fact, the biggest problem of the day seemed to centre around a mysterious noise emanating from the engine of one of the bikes. I listened myself, but with the racket from the exhaust I could hear absolutely nothing.

The other Angels sat around in the sun, or cleaned their bikes . . . or had sex with their mommas. It was all rather strange.

I was just getting really hungry, when the Angels suddenly became alert. The sun was setting, and the evening chill was beginning to set in. Then Hick stood up, and looked expectantly up the unmade track towards the road. I stood with him, wondering what was going to happen. I saw the glare of headlights, heard the crescendoing sound of unsilenced engines, smelt the fumes of the exhaust blowing in ahead of them on the chill wind from the moors.

I started counting, then gave up . . . for in a while more than a hundred Hell's Angels had joined us on the beach.

'We still waiting?' I shouted at Hick over the racket of the engines.

'No Sal . . . we ain't. . . .'

That night was a wild and dangerous scene. The new Angels had brought vast quantities of food and beer with them . . . and drugs. Almost as soon as they'd arrived, the reefers appeared. Not little thin handmades that I'd sometimes seen in the past, but great fat joints, bursting with the green substance. They were passed round freely, and I smoked my share.

I was used to the company of the Angels now, though their appearance was still alarming. I was no nearer to understanding them, but at least I had learned how to live with them. In a nutshell: say nothing, do nothing, and about once an hour make some flattering remark about the bikes.

Hick was in a fantastic mood. Once he'd eaten, his taciturn state wore off, and he walked round with me chewing the fat with some of the other Angels. I realised that he was leader only of the eighteen Angels who had come to the camp. In this large crowd he was high on the pecking order, but not top.

The night wore on, and I grew tired. The Angels shouted, sang, told hair-raising tales of burns along the Great West Road. All the while, the mommas held tight to their Angels' arms, just as I stayed by Hick. I was too frightened to leave him.

Only once was there a hint of trouble. One of the new Angels had been watching me for some time, obviously watching the swell of my breasts beneath my tee-shirt, the protuberant buds of my nipples. In the end, he came over to me, ignoring Hick, and put an arm around my waist. His hand went up and closed over my breast, and his mouth came down to kiss me. I smelt the beer on his breath, felt the harsh rasp of his unshaven face.

Hick moved.

He snatched the Angel's hand from my breast, and with his other hand took him by the throat and propelled him backwards. The other Angel's feet tripped on a piece of rock, and they both fell over onto the sand.

Hick was on his feet first, and a knife had appeared in his hand.

'One more fucking move like that. . . .'

'OK, OK. Just gettin' friendly.'

A crowd of the Angels was gathering.

'Just get unfriendly, brother. She's with me.'

'OK, OK,' the other Angel said again.

Hick stared down at him, then on an impulse kicked him once and hard in the side. The Angel doubled up in pain, and there was a roar of approval from those watching.

'Anyone else wanta make a move at her?'

To my surprise, and not exactly pleasure, several of the Angels made scathing remarks about my appearance and figure. 'Flat-chested bint . . . too fucking pale . . . thick as two planks. . . .' Et bloody cetera. I wondered how Hick would take this, but he seemed pleased. Perhaps it was the Angels' way of saying they'd leave me alone.

That was evidently what it was, for the crowd dissolved as quickly as it had formed, and the Angel who'd made the move at me, got to his feet and limped off.

I saw him later on, making love to one of the mommas, so I guess he wasn't too dissatisfied with the way things worked out in the end.

After this incident, Hick took me aside, and I walked off with him to a lonely part of the beach. Tacitly, I was his girl now. He had fought for me, and I was his. I wasn't sure I exactly approved of the system, but I couldn't see any way of bucking it.

Of all the Angels I had met, I disapproved least of Hick. He shared many of the unpleasant aspects of all Angels, but there was something indefinable that set him apart. I tried asking him questions about his past, but either he was inarticulate or he pretended to be, for I learnt nothing.

Alone with him, I sat down on the sand. Stubbornly, a memory came to me of the last time I had been alone on a beach with a man . . . but I thrust it aside.

Hick possessed little sexual finesse. He pulled my tee-shirt off, and began to press and massage my breasts as if they were bread-dough. I laid back on the sand, and forced myself to relax. I waited while he pulled off the rest of my clothes, then dropped his trousers. Hick made love savagely and selfishly, and I was incapable of enjoying it. He was the worst kind of lover: semi-brutal, caring nothing for his partner. But I didn't try to stop him. A few minutes later, I pulled on my clothes and we walked back to the others.

That night, he made love to me again. It was no worse, perhaps marginally better.

CHAPTER 13

In the morning, I said to Hick: 'What are we doing now?'

'Security,' he said, and wouldn't enlarge.

Half an hour later, we were on the road again, heading west. The Angels stayed off the main roads, keeping instead to narrow lanes that ran along the coast. Soon we had left Devon, and were in Cornwall. The scenery grew wilder, more rugged. It struck me as strange territory for the Angels, but they appeared to know where they were going.

There were more and more people on the roads, and as we roared past they took no notice of us. I wondered why, for I knew that most people were frightened by the appearance of Hell's Angels. And then I realised: most of the people we saw were young, and dressed casually. More mystery, for Cornwall is very much a holiday centre for families. It looked like Hyde

Park on a hot Sunday afternoon, when the Rolling Stones gave a free concert, or that flower-power rally I'd been to a few years before.

And it was then that I began to understand where we were heading.

The Angels brought their bikes to a halt on the brow of a hill. The view from here was beautiful . . . looking west across a vista of rocky cliffs, blue sea and white surf.

'That's it, ain't it?' one of the Angels said to Hick.

'That's right.'

I looked in the direction they were pointing, and saw a small island a few hundred yards from the shore. The tide was out, and it was possible to walk out across the sand to it.

And doing just that were hundreds or thousands of young people.

Hick revved his engine, and we shot forward, travelling far faster than we had done so far that day. The other Angels kept up with him. The road descended sharply, winding its way down to the beach. At the bottom of the hill, the road took a sharp turn and started up again, but Hick flung the bike across the verge, down a short slope and onto the sand. Now he held the throttle wide open, and we accelerated quickly, throwing up a cloud of sand and spray. Ahead of us, the young people walking stepped to one side to make way for us.

The island was dead ahead of us. The tide had not quite exposed it, and for the last hundred yards or so we splashed through the shallows, spray from the Angel's bike in front of us drenching us both.

Then we reached the island, and lurched up a rock-strewn grass slope.

The top of the island was flat and wide, and a gate had been erected across the logical entrance from the shore. Several men stood there wearing white armbands, and the young people queued up to pay their entrance fees. The Angels did not stop, roaring towards the gap as if no barrier existed. Once more, the people stepped with alacrity out of our way, and the Angels shot through.

There, on the wide expanse of wind-blown grass, laid or sat tens of thousands of young people. And from a stage made of scaffolding and tarpaulins, rock music blared from speakers. A pop-group was preparing to start a gig. The smell of pot wafted from a thousand illicit joints. Peddlers of underground magazines wandered through the crowds. Hot-dog stalls served long hungry queues.

And now the Angels were here to act as security-guards. . . .

As we drew up behind the stage, someone turned off the record, and the group began their first number. A hundred and fifty decibels of rock music blared out at the waiting crowd, across the beach to where the latecomers still walked or waded towards the island, and across the most rugged and beautiful coastline in Britain.

'This your first pop-festival, Sal?'

'Yes.'

'You'll be OK with us.'

'Thanks.'

Hick was in his element. With the other Angels, he sorted out the 'security' arrangements they were unofficially 'providing', and once again the Angels became a threatening and paramilitary force, walking round the festival in groups, holding their clubs or wrenches in a terrifying manner. They took over control of the entrance gate, kept the pop-fans from coming too close to the stage, and acted as protectors to the several groups who were already there.

But I had had enough of Hick and his friends. I wanted to get away from them, before I became too involved. They had served their purpose in getting me away from the camp, but now I wanted to get back to my former life. In short, I wanted to go home. . . .

The festival provided a perfect escape. I could lose myself in the crowd in seconds.

I said to Hick: 'I'm just going to the loo.'

'Yeah.'

I walked off in the direction of a large tent, where a long line of girls stood waiting patiently to go inside. I had gone a few yards, when I looked back at Hick. He had turned away, and was talking to several of the other Angels.

At once, I moved in another direction, walking deliberately through the most crowded part of the field. It took me about ten minutes to get across to the entrance, and I slipped out. I ran down the slope to the water's edge.

But the tide had come in. . . . I found myself looking across several hundreds yards of white surf. It was completely impractical for me even to consider trying to wade or swim to the mainland.

I noticed that there were still several hundred fans on the

beach across the water. And they were coming over to the island on boats. I watched for a few minutes until one of the boats came up to the island and discharged its passengers.

'Are you going back to the beach?' I said to the boatman.

He nodded. 'A pound.'

'What?'

'It'll cost you a pound, miss. That's the fare.'

'But I haven't got a pound!'

'OK.' He turned, and cast off the rope. He chugged calmly back towards the beach to collect his next boatload of pop-happy fans.

I hung around for a few minutes, and asked several boatmen if they'd take me back. All were willing to do so . . . for a price. And I simply had no money on me. Obviously, the locals were as opportunistic as everyone else when a pop-festival landed itself in the neighbourhood. They knew that once people were on the island they'd be helpless to get off without boats, and they had the boats. . . .

I was a virtual prisoner on the island until the next low tide, which wouldn't be until late that evening.

There was no choice but to stay put on the island until then. Mentally reconciled to the idea, I thought I may as well go and enjoy myself. The sun was hot, the scenery was beautiful, the music was loud.

Then another unpleasant thought crossed my mind. I had to get back into the actual site of the festival . . . and I had no money. I followed the latest boatload of fans up to the entrance, trying to think up some desperate scheme for bluffing my way in. Perhaps I could find some way up if I worked round the island.

But the venue had been chosen carefully. This side of the island was the only slope; on all other sides were steep, crumbly cliffs. The path up from the beach led through a narrow cleft, and it was here that the gate had been placed.

In desperation I was fomenting some plan of pleading my way in . . . and then I realised that nothing like that would be necessary. The Angels had taken over the gate, and I knew the particular Angel standing to one side. It was the one who had made the pass at me the night before.

I walked straight up to him.

I said: 'Hi.'

' 'Ullo.'

'Hey . . . I'm sorry about last night. I was sorry Hick fought you off, because I was fancying you.'

'That so?'

I nodded. 'Why not try again tonight? I'll make sure Hick doesn't find out.'

He grinned broadly. While I was talking, I had stepped round him.

He said: 'OK.'

I said: 'OK . . . .'

He was still grinning as I walked in to the field. Now I was inside, I quickly lost myself in the crowd. I was amazed how many people were here. It was quite a large island, and yet the area in front of the stage was packed. It was an excellent site for a festival. When festivals were held on the mainland, the local residents quite rightly objected to the noise and the thousands of people; here, the festival was miles from the nearest village, and no one was inconvenienced except the festival-goers themselves. If they didn't mind spending three days on a lump of rock a few hundred yards out in the Atlantic Ocean – and they didn't – then nobody else minded.

It was odd, though, for once again I had found myself in a situation not unlike that of the camp. A group of people, cutting themselves off for a few days from the outside world, escaping from normal mundane problems. The island was virtually self-contained for the period of the festival. There was food, company, sanitation, entertainment. No one in their right minds would consider being here permanently, but then no one wanted to escape permanently, as I had learned to my own satisfaction.

I wandered through the camping area, where dozens of tents had been erected. Even here the music was loud, but when I emerged into the area where people sat or laid, it was deafening.

I worked my way to as near the front as I could manage, and sat down on the grass. A few seconds later, a pot cigarette was passed to me, I took a drag and passed it on.

The group was finishing its set. I didn't particularly care for the music; it was 'heavy' rock, and the organist in particular seemed intent on swamping us all with his music. Finally, they came to their last number, and then more records were played.

The next group was . . . much to my surprise . . . Ess Pry, and I settled down to enjoy them with more leisure than I had been able to find a couple of nights before.

They sounded different in the open air . . . less rowdy, though just as earthy and funky. It took them a few numbers to get the crowd on their side, but by the fifth number, which was a screaming rock chant, everyone was on their feet cheering their heads off.

The rest of their set was highly enjoyable, but of course it had to end. And then there were more records.

The next group that appeared was Maxima Culpa.

They were four bars in to their first number before I recognised them. Alan was there: slimmer, longer hair, more relaxed than I had ever seen him. And he was playing better, if anything, than the first time I had seen him.

I forgot the crowd of thousands around me. I forgot the rest of the group. It was just Alan and me, and we were alone.

I stood up, stepped over the other people in front and moved forward, uncaring of the shouts of 'Sit down!' that followed me. Soon I was as near to the stage as it was possible to get, and I stood there in a swaying mass of fans, staring fixedly at Alan, willing him to see me.

From where he stood I must have been just another fan, just another face in the crowd. But my attention was riveted on him, knowing that this time he would not up and leave me. The hurt he had caused me was gone. He didn't yet know it, but he had returned to me, and this time it was on his own terms.

Only once I took my eyes off him, and that was when the crush of the crowd around me was growing intolerable. I saw that now most people were standing up, pushing forward in their excitement. For if Ess Pry had been good, Maxima Culpa were magnificently good. And it was on Alan and his guitar that the group centred.

Their act had changed. Before, Maxima Culpa had been a good group musically, but visually they had been like most others. They had stood at their instruments and played them. But in the months since Alan had joined them, there had been a lot of work put into changing this. Maxima Culpa were better musically, and they looked better. They moved about the stage almost as if the music was forcing them to. Alan looked tormented, sweat pouring down his face, and soaking into his shirt. The drummer hammered his skins, as if he hated them with every bone in his body. The other guitarists moved with Alan, throwing back their long hair as it fell across their faces. The total result was indescribably exciting . . . and the crowd was responding. At the end of each number, the cheering was long and loud, and as Alan announced the following number a burst of appreciative applause followed. While I had been languishing in the camp, it was clear that Maxima Culpa had been earning a reputation.

Then, far too early for my liking, Maxima Culpa came to their last number.

'Goodbye everybody!' Alan shouted into the microphone, took off his guitar, and leaned it against an amplifier. Then he followed the others as they disappeared behind the stage.

He hadn't noticed me. . . .

Or perhaps he had chosen not to. . . .

Frustration and anguish rose in me. I couldn't let him slip away this time. . . .

The pressure of the crowd was easing, as more people went back to sit down again on the grass. I found myself able to move, and desperately I worked my way towards the side of the stage. There was a long metal barrier here, to prevent the fans from getting to the area behind the stage. I looked round, could see no way past it. I couldn't climb it – it was too high and too solidly built for that – and I couldn't get round it. The only way through was by a removable section that was presently closed.

I leant against it, trying to find some way of pushing it back. A padlock was there, solid and unmovable.

There was a noise overhead, and I looked up. A helicopter was hovering over the site, and coming down to land in the area behind the stage. Irrationally I knew it had come to collect Maxima Culpa . . . and Alan. There was no logical reason for this assumption, but in my desperation I could think of no other reason for its presence.

I saw Hick.

'Hick! *Hick!*'

He didn't hear me; the noise from the amplified record was too great. He was about twenty yards from me, marching towards the cluster of tents where the groups were allowed to wait before they went on stage. Over his shoulder he held a heavy spanner.

'*HICK!!*'

He turned, and saw me at last. He stared for a second, uncomprehendingly, then it sunk in. He walked over to me with an agonising sloth.

'Sal . . . what you doin' there?'

'I got lost,' I said. 'Can you let me in?'

He looked dumbly at the padlock.

'Needs a key, Sal.'

'Have you got it?'

He shook his head slowly. 'Have to borrer it from one of the others. Wait here.'

I waited. He walked off slowly, and stopped to talk to one of the other Angels. I was swearing with anxiety now, for I saw that the helicopter had landed, and was now parked in the group area, its blades circling slowly. There was a lot of movement around it, and a group was unloading a lot of gear. With every moment that passed, my certainty that it had come to whisk away Alan and the rest of the group grew greater. Still I had no rational reason for believing this, but even so there was no quieting the awful feeling.

It wouldn't have been so bad if I had thought that Alan knew I was here. His simple ignorance of my presence was the frustration. If he knew I was here, and still wanted to leave, then that was fair enough. If he knew I was here, and wanted to stay, then that was how I wanted it. But the awful possibility of our paths crossing so closely, yet not actually meeting, was more than I could stand.

Hick was still talking to the other Angel, and I banged my fist against the fence in my impatience.

'Hurry, Hick,' I said under my breath. 'For God's sake . . . *hurry!*'

But he was taking his time. Perhaps this Angel was the one with the key, I thought desperately.

But no. . . . After a few more minutes, Hick wandered off aimlessly. He walked a few paces in one direction, then stopped. He looked round as if he was trying to remember something.

'*The key,*' I hissed at him, knowing he'd never hear.

The helicopter's blades were still rotating, and the group had nearly got all of its gear out. There were several people hanging around, and from the distance it was impossible for me to tell what was happening.

I was wondering what more direct action I could take, instead of standing there helplessly, when I saw Hick move purposefully towards one of the organisers. I saw Hick point vaguely in my direction, and the man shook his head.

To my unspeakable fury, Hick shrugged and came over in my direction.

'Did you get the key?' I said.

'They . . . don't know where it is. Know what I mean?'

'No I don't. For God's sake, Hick . . . you've got to let me through!'

'Wait here, an' I'll see what I can do.'

Before I could say anything, he wandered off again, leaving me standing there once more. I could have died with frustration.

And then all my worst expectations were confirmed. I saw five young men walking over to the helicopter, and one of them was wearing a bright red tee-shirt, identical to the one in which Alan had been playing. I didn't need any further confirmation, I *knew* it was Alan.

Once more I shook the fence, hoping illogically that I could somehow loosen the padlock.

'Wanta get in?'

It was another of the Angels.

'Yes! Have you got the key?'

Two hundred yards away, I could see the last of the young men climbing into the helicopter, and a few seconds later the hatch was closed.

'Somewhere here. . . .' He started going through his pockets.

'Hurry,' I pleaded. '*Please* hurry!'

After what seemed like an eternity of searching, he produced the key and fitted it into the padlock. I saw the rotor-blades of the helicopter start to move round more quickly.

I practically burst open the gate, and barged through.

'Thanks!' I shouted, and ran for all my life in the direction of the helicopter.

The pilot revved his engine, and the blades whipped round invisibly. I was still only halfway there. . . . And then, slowly at first, and quickly later, the helicopter lifted off.

Still I ran on, knowing I was already too late. My legs felt as if they were coated in lead, my muscles as if they were asleep. I pumped my limbs harder, but without apparent effect.

The helicopter was now about twenty feet off the ground, and its nose dipped round and the machine began to move off in an easterly direction.

I ran on, knowing it was hopeless. I was staring up at the machine, blinded as it flew between me and the sun.

At last I stopped, and stood there panting. My whole body was aching, and my breath rasped in an out as if my throat were lined with sandpaper. In a stupid way, I took the time to notice that my breasts were hurting from being bounced around when I was running.

The helicopter was now about a quarter of a mile away from me, and heading towards the mainland.

I began to cry. *Oh Alan. . . .*

For a few seconds I covered my face with my hands, and let

the tears flow. Then, for my last sight of the helicopter, I looked up and stood there in the sunlight, trying to see through my watery eyes. It was now more than a mile away from the island . . . and circling round. . . .

It was *circling*. . . .

I could no longer count on fortune, and simply stood there accepting that it did indeed appear to be turning back. Perhaps those on board wanted one last look at the festival site . . . or someone had forgotten something. I began jumping up and down, waving my arms in the air.

Unmistakably, the helicopter was returning, and it was coming back to where I was standing. Thirty seconds later, it blotted out the sun as it hovered ten yards away from me. The pilot brought it down to a gentle landing . . . the hatch was opened . . . and then a red-shirted figure was stumbling across the uneven surface towards me.

'Sally! I *thought* it was you. . . .'

'Alan!'

'But what are you doing here?'

'Alan. . . .'

And then I was in his arms, and he was kissing me and I was crying again. He held me tight, and I clung to him. I was aware of nothing else. Alan was my world.

Later:

'Why didn't you tell me you were going?'

'I . . . didn't want to. I knew I'd meet you again, I just knew it. But I was afraid you'd try to stop me.'

'No, Alan . . . no . . . .'

He hugged me again, and we kissed.

Later:

We became aware that there was a helicopter a few feet away from us, and that there were several grinning faces watching us.

Alan looked embarrassed. 'Er . . . Sally, you'd better meet the rest of the band.'

He led me over to the helicopter, and we climbed inside. The hatch was closed, and Alan introduced me to the others. From somewhere, a bottle was produced and opened, and only much later I realised that the helicopter had taken off again, and we were several thousand feet in the air.

I snuggled down into Alan's arms as we sped on into the evening . . . towards London, towards home, and towards a lifetime of happiness. . . .

EPILOGUE

'AND you married him and lived happily ever after.'

I opened my eyes.

'Eh?'

'Alan. You got married?'

'Who? Got what?'

'Married. No, wait a minute. I see now. . . .'

I blinked at him. Slowly I realised that this was Trevor. I moved slightly, and felt the water-bed squishing beneath me.

'Just stay relaxed for a moment. I'll get you a drink. Scotch and soda all right?'

'Yes please.'

I lay back and stared at the ceiling. It was weird and disorienting. I could still see a face before me, but it was no one's I recognised.

'Here.' Trevor handed me the drink. 'Now, tell me. Does anything else follow? What happened, for instance, when you got back to London?'

I felt – and looked – blank.

'Did you ever hear from Doreen again?'

'Who?'

'Your friend at the camp.'

'Oh . . . Doreen. No, I don't think I did.' I frowned. 'It all seems a bit blank, I'm afraid.'

'Would you like me to replay the tapes to jog your memory a bit?'

I remembered what had happened the last time he did that.

'No thank you,' I said.

'Now then, Sally. There are a few loose ends. You never said, for instance, in which town this holiday-camp was situated.'

'That's right. I didn't.'

'Well . . .?'

'I'm afraid I haven't the faintest idea.'

'But it was in Devon?'

'I suppose so.'

He scribbled something in his notebook.

'Your parents. Did they ever get back your belongings?'

Blank.

'You asked Doreen to send them on.'

'Oh yes.'

'I see.' Trevor was beginning to develop a frown. 'Well . . . all I can say is that we appear to have overcome the amnesia.'

'So I'm all right now?'

'It's hard to say. Certainly, your powers of description at certain times were – well – graphic, shall we say?'

I looked at my watch. It was getting late.

'Trevor . . . ?'

'Yes?'

'I don't want to disappoint you, but I don't *feel* cured. All that stuff in the camp was . . . I don't know. It felt like a memory, but it doesn't seem to relate in any way to me. For instance, I've a clear conception of the "Mum" and "Dad" I told you about . . . but they're nothing like my real Mum and Dad. And Alan. From what I remember of him, I had the biggest crush in the world any girl could have had. And he had one on me too. But . . . I don't know an Alan. In fact, I don't think I've ever met anyone of that name. And the only pop-festival I've ever been to was . . . Oh!'

'Something the matter?'

'I've just remembered,' I said slowly, 'I once went to a pop-festival on Salisbury plain. . . .'

'But the one you've just described to me was in Cornwall.'

'Oh that!' I said scathingly. 'I've never been to Cornwall. I was just making that up.'

'I beg your pardon?'

'Granted,' I said cheekily. 'I've just realised . . . I invented that.'

'What do you mean.'

'Well look at it this way,' I said. 'After Alan left the camp I had no way of meeting him . . . right? I knew he was in a pop-group, so wasn't it logical that he'd be at a pop-festival? OK . . . so I arranged for those Hell's Angels to come along and whip me off to the nearest pop-festival I could think of.

'Anyway,' I went on, 'if you knew anything about anything, you'd know that pop-festivals aren't like that now.'

Trevor stood up.

'Are you trying to tell me, Sally, that you made all this up?' He gestured towards the tape-recorder.

'I suppose so.'

He shook his head sadly. 'Then we're back to square one.'

I stood up too, leaving the water-bed rather regretfully.

'No we're not,' I said. 'Because it's done the trick. Since I've told you all that, I've realised that I can remember everything I'd lost.'

He looked at me sharply.

'Do you mean that?'

'Yes of course.'

Suddenly, his expression was more serious.

'Look, Sally, I hope you haven't been wasting my time. If as you say everything you've told me was an invention, and now you have had your memory restored – by what appears on the face of it to be a miracle – then I suspect that you never had amnesia at all.'

I became alarmed by his serious manner. 'Trevor . . . I assure you, I really did lose my memory.'

'But now it's back.'

'Yes!'

'And you maintain that this elaborate tale about a holiday-camp was mere invention?'

'Yes!' I stared at him earnestly. 'I didn't intend to deceive you. When I started, it felt as if it was real. But now it's all finished . . . well, I can't relate it to anything in reality. And because I was trying to compare it with what I know is real, I suddenly found that I could remember! It hasn't come back in patches . . . it's as if it had never gone.'

Trevor frowned, and turned away.

'Then my original thesis was accurate. You *have* been in a fugue condition. The fugue didn't take you back to earlier incidents from your own life, but created a whole sequence of events that directly paralleled your real life. Would you say that was a fair estimate?'

'Yes.'

'And your real memories . . .?'

I grinned at him. 'I think I'd like to keep those to myself.'

He grinned back. 'Sally, my dear, if they are anything like your inventions, then perhaps I understand why.'

'Good.'

'In which case, if you say you are now cured I see no reason to detain you. I can write a discharge-note to the hospital, and you need be bothered no more.'

'I'm cured?'

'Yes. I wish that every case were as clear-cut. And, may I add, as entertaining.'

He took my arm, and led me through the outer office to the hallway. Outside, the corridor was cool and semi-dark. He switched on lights, and led me down the stairs.

'You will, of course, allow me to drive you home?'

'Yes please,' I said.

At the door, he stopped.

'Sally, don't think me impertinent, but may I make a suggestion? From listening to your story, I must say that you have a strong flair for fiction. Have you ever had any desire to write?'

I shook my head. 'That's for intellectuals.'

'No it's not. Quite ordinary people write books, you know. You have a good sense of narrative, an excellent eye for detail and – well – a healthy imagination. You should put it to a good use.'

I wasn't sure whether he was trying to flatter me, or whether he genuinely meant it.

'You're just saying that,' I said.

'No I'm not. Wait here a minute.' He turned, and galloped up the stairs two at a time. In a couple of minutes he was back. 'Here . . . take these. You might find them useful one day.'

He had thrust several flat boxes into my hands.

'What are they?' I said, genuinely puzzled.

'The tapes. Rattling good tale, I would say.'

And so he drove me home, and Mum and Dad were waiting up for me, and I pronounced myself cured.

Well . . . Trevor had a point. The tapes *did* make quite a tale, but before I got around to those there were my *real* memories to get rid of.*

And so Sally Deenes, one-time hitch-hiker, one-time drifter and one-time amnesiac, became a writer.

It made a change, anyway. But now that's me and my life up to date, I've got the future to consider. I've sort of run of out memories – false or otherwise – and so I've got to find something new.

I wonder what would happen if . . .?

* See *Hitch-Hiker* (1971) and *The New Drifters* (1972) by Petra Christian, New English Library.

SEX MANNERS FOR THE YOUNG GENERATION

by Robert Chartham

Speaking in the language of today, Robert Chartham, a marriage guidance counsellor and best-selling author of SEX MANNERS FOR MEN and SEX MANNERS FOR ADVANCED LOVERS, now gives frank advice to the generation growing up in this world of change.

So many young people are confused by the present tide of permissiveness and sexual liberation that essentials such as contraception, hygiene and personal moral tensions are too often forgotten.

Here is a sympathetic and informed reminder of what it means to mature in a youth-orientated society. All topics are discussed, in all honesty.

This is the book that all young people have been looking for.

NEW ENGLISH LIBRARY

SUEDEHEAD
by Richard Allen

A young and brutal bovver boy called Joe Hawkins
caused outrage when he was first introduced to the world
in the New English Library smash hit SKINHEAD.

Now Joe has grown his hair and swapped his boots and
braces for a velvet-collared Abercrombie coat. His aggro
days are over ... but his city-slicker days are just
beginning.

SUEDEHEAD is the sequel to the bestselling SKINHEAD,
and by the same author is THE BOOT BOYS – with yet
more trouble on the terraces!

NEW ENGLISH LIBRARY

NEL BESTSELLERS

Crime

T013 332	CLOUDS OF WITNESS	*Dorothy L. Sayers* 40p
T016 307	THE UNPLEASANTNESS AT THE BELLONA CLUB	*Dorothy L. Sayers* 40p
W003 011	GAUDY NIGHT	*Dorothy L. Sayers* 40p
T010 457	THE NINE TAILORS	*Dorothy L. Sayers* 35p
T012 484	FIVE RED HERRINGS	*Dorothy L. Sayers* 40p
T015 556	MURDER MUST ADVERTISE	*Dorothy L. Sayers* 40p

Fiction

W002 775	HATTER'S CASTLE	*A. J. Cronin* 60p
T013 944	CRUSADER'S TOMB	*A. J. Cronin* 60p
T013 936	THE JUDAS TREE	*A. J. Cronin* 50p
T001 288	THE TROUBLE WITH LAZY ETHEL	*Ernest K. Gann* 30p
T003 922	IN THE COMPANY OF EAGLES	*Ernest K. Gann* 30p
W002 145	THE NINTH DIRECTIVE	*Adam Hall* 25p
T012 271	THE WARSAW DOCUMENT	*Adam Hall* 40p
T012 778	QUEEN IN DANGER	*Adam Hall* 30p
T007 243	SYLVIA SCARLETT	*Compton Mackenzie* 30p
T007 669	SYLVIA AND ARTHUR	*Compton Mackenzie* 30p
T007 677	SYLVIA AND MICHAEL	*Compton Mackenzie* 35p
T009 084	SIR, YOU BASTARD	*G. F. Newman* 30p
T009 769	THE HARRAD EXPERIMENT	*Robert H. Rimmer* 40p
T010 252	THE REBELLION OF YALE MARRATT	*Robert H. Rimmer* 40p
T013 820	THE DREAM MERCHANTS	*Harold Robbins* 75p
T012 255	THE CARPETBAGGERS	*Harold Robbins* 80p
T016 560	WHERE LOVE HAS GONE	*Harold Robbins* 75p
T013 707	THE ADVENTURERS	*Harold Robbins* 80p
T006 743	THE INHERITORS	*Harold Robbins* 60p
T009 467	STILETTO	*Harold Robbins* 30p
T015 289	NEVER LEAVE ME	*Harold Robbins* 40p
T016 579	NEVER LOVE A STRANGER	*Harold Robbins* 75p
T011 798	A STONE FOR DANNY FISHER	*Harold Robbins* 60p
T015 874	79 PARK AVENUE	*Harold Robbins* 60p
T011 461	THE BETSY	*Harold Robbins* 75p
T010 201	RICH MAN, POOR MAN	*Irwin Shaw* 80p
W002 186	THE PLOT	*Irving Wallace* 75p
T009 718	THE THREE SIRENS	*Irving Wallace* 75p
T010 341	THE PRIZE	*Irving Wallace* 80p

Historical

T009 750	THE WARWICK HEIRESS	*Margaret Abbey* 30p
T013 731	KNIGHT WITH ARMOUR	*Alfred Duggan* 40p
T013 758	THE LADY FOR RANSOM	*Alfred Duggan* 40p
T011 585	THE ROSE IN SPRING	*Eleanor Fairburn* 30p
T009 734	RICHMOND AND ELIZABETH	*Brenda Honeyman* 30p
T011 593	HARRY THE KING	*Brenda Honeyman* 35p
T009 742	THE ROSE BOTH RED AND WHITE	*Betty King* 30p
T010 988	BRIDE OF LIBERTY	*Frank Yerby* 30p
T014 649	FAIROAKS	*Frank Yerby* 50p
T014 045	TREASURE OF PLEASANT VALLEY	*Frank Yerby* 35p

Science Fiction

T011 410	EARTHWORKS	*Brian Aldiss* 25p
T014 576	THE INTERPRETER	*Brian Aldiss* 30p
T014 347	SPACE RANGER	*Isaac Asimov* 30p
T016 900	STRANGER IN A STRANGE LAND	*Robert Heinlein* 75p
W002 908	STAR BEAST	*Robert Heinlein* 30p
T011 534	I WILL FEAR NO EVIL	*Robert Heinlein* 75p
W002 684	THE HEAVEN MAKERS	*Frank Herbert* 30p
T011 844	DUNE	*Frank Herbert* 75p

T012 298	DUNE MESSIAH	Frank Herbert 40p
T012 859	QUEST FOR THE FUTURE	A. E. Van Vogt 35p
T015 270	THE WEAPON MAKERS	A. E. Van Vogt 30p

War

T012 964	COLDITZ: THE GERMAN STORY	Reinhold Eggers 40p
T009 890	THE K BOATS	Don Everitt 30p
T013 324	THE GOOD SHEPHERD	C. S. Forester 35p
W002 484	THE FLEET THAT HAD TO DIE	Richard Hough 25p
W002 805	HUNTING OF FORCE Z	Richard Hough 30p
T012 999	P.Q. 17 – CONVOY TO HELL	Lund & Ludlam 30p
T011 755	TRAWLERS GO TO WAR	Lund & Ludlam 40p
T010 872	BLACK SATURDAY	Alexander McKee 30p
T010 074	THE GREEN BERET	Hilary St. George Saunders 40p
T010 066	THE RED BERET	Hilary St. George Saunders 40p

Western

T016 994	EDGE: No. 1: THE LONER	George Gilman 30p
T016 986	EDGE: No. 2: TEN THOUSAND DOLLARS AMERICAN	George Gilman 30p
T010 929	EDGE: No. 3: APACHE DEATH	George Gilman 25p
T017 001	EDGE: No. 4: KILLER'S BREED	George Gilman 30p
T016 536	EDGE: No. 5: BLOOD ON SILVER	George Gilman 30p
T013 774	EDGE: No. 6: THE BLUE, THE GREY AND THE RED	George Gilman 25p

General

T011 763	SEX MANNERS FOR MEN	Robert Chartham 30p
W002 531	SEX MANNERS FOR ADVANCED LOVERS	Robert Chartham 25p
W002 835	SEX AND THE OVER FORTIES	Robert Chartham 30p
T010 732	THE SENSUOUS COUPLE	Dr. 'C' 25p
P002 367	AN ABZ OF LOVE	Inge and Stem Hegeler 60p
P011 402	A HAPPIER SEX LIFE	Dr. Sha Kokken 70p
W002 584	SEX MANNERS FOR SINGLE GIRLS	Georges Valensin 25p
W002 592	THE FRENCH ART OF SEX MANNERS	Georges Valensin 25p
W002 726	THE POWER TO LOVE	E. W. Hirsch M.D. 47½p

Mad

S004 708	VIVA MAD!	30p
S004 676	MAD'S DON MARTIN COMES ON STRONG	30p
S004 816	MAD'S DAVE BERG LOOKS AT SICK WORLD	30p
S005 078	MADVERTISING	30p
S004 987	MAD SNAPPY ANSWERS TO STUPID QUESTIONS	30p

NEL P.O. BOX 11, FALMOUTH, CORNWALL

Please send cheque or postal order. Allow 6p per book to cover postage and packing.

Name ....

Address ....

....

Title ....
(APRIL)